P9-CDB-733

Blessing's Bead

Debby Dahl Edwardson

BLESSING'S BEAD

MELANIE KROUPA BOOKS
FARRAR, STRAUS AND GIROUX
NEW YORK

Blessing's Bead is a work of fiction. While many of the historical events did occur, the characters themselves are fictional. I have given these characters real Iñupiaq names, but the personal histories attached to those names are entirely fictional.

Copyright © 2009 by Debby Dahl Edwardson
Printed in July 2009 in the United States of America
by RR Donnelley, Harrisonburg, VA
Distributed in Canada by Douglas & McIntyre Ltd.
Designed by Jay Colvin
First edition, 2009
1   3   5   7   9   10   8   6   4   2

www.fsgkidsbooks.com

Library of Congress Cataloging-in-Publication Data
Edwardson, Debby Dahl.
     Blessing's bead / Debby Dahl Edwardson.— 1st ed.
         p.   cm.
     Summary: In 1917, Aaluk leaves for Siberia while her sister Nutaaq
remains in their Alaskan village and becomes one of the few survivors
of an influenza epidemic, then in 1986, Nutaaq's great-granddaughter
leaves her mother due to a different kind of sickness and returns to
the village where they were born.
     ISBN: 978-0-374-30805-6
     1. Inupiat—Juvenile fiction.   [1. Inupiat—Fiction.   2. Family life—
Alaska—Fiction.   3. Villages—Fiction.   4. Tundras—Fiction.   5. Influenza—
Fiction.   6. Alcoholism—Fiction.   7. Alaska—History—1867–1959—Fiction.
8. Alaska—History—1959— —Fiction.]   I. Title.

PZ7.E2657 Ble 2009
[Fic]—dc22

                                                                    2008026726

Photograph on page ix courtesy of Library of Congress, LC-USZ62-135998

For my mother,
Sue Dahl Foss (1914–2007),
who taught me
the enduring power of love

We are named for those who have passed on. Our names come with their own kinship, their own memories. We make our families strong that way—through the power of our names. This is how it was in the old days and how it still is, even today. Some things never change.

FAMILY TREE*

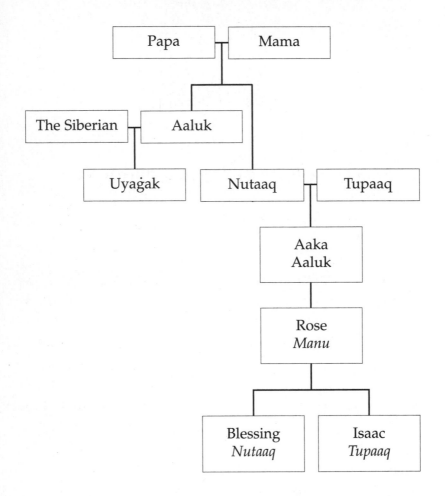

*Iñupiaq families are very large, with many brothers, sisters, cousins, aunts, uncles, *ataatas* (great-uncles), *aanas* (great-aunts), and *amaus* (great-, great-great-, and great-great-great-aunts, -uncles, and -grandparents). There is not enough room to show all of Blessing's family here; this family tree shows only some of the family members that you will meet in this book.

Grandma Aaluk Remembers
1989

*M*y *old eyes, they like frosty windows. Can't see out, sometimes, only in. But some kinds of pictures stay inside, bright
as spring sun on the ocean ice.*

*This is one of those pictures—a photo of my father and mother,
your great-grandparents. Sure, I remember it. Nutaaq, my mother
—she's the one you were named after. The one who survived. You
can see how it's marked her, can't you? It's there in the way she
holds her fingers, real tight, and in her eyes, even when she smiles.
Like the shadow of a cloud, far out on the tundra, right before it
rains.*

Some kinds of sadness never do let go.

•

T H E Y L I V E D *on one of the islands in those days, my mother,
Nutaaq, and my aunt, Aaluk—the one I was named for. The Sibe-*

rian Eskimos used to come often, traveling across the open ocean from the Russian coast to the Alaskan side. Traveling in the summer months, come east to trade.

I see them in my mind's eye, even now—Nutaaq and her elder sister, Aaluk—standing together on the cliff side of the island, gazing out to sea with bright young eyes, watching for the sails of the Siberians. They are dreaming, as young girls do, of things to come, wondering what lies on the far side of that ocean horizon.

Nutaaq imagines mountains as tall as the moon and Aaluk pictures them full of flowers. Flowers as purple as the night sky, just before sunrise.

Aaluk has a tattoo on her chin, the kind they used in the old days to mark a girl's passage into womanhood: three fine lines of soot stitched straight and smooth with an ivory needle. And that tattoo is yet so new she's afraid to even smile for fear of marring it.

This is how I imagine them: two sisters, standing together on an island cliff, dark hair waving in the wind. Waiting.

If I close my eyes, I can even hear them speak, just as they speak in Nutaaq's stories. For my mother, Nutaaq, was a real storyteller. When Nutaaq tells this story, you can almost smell the smoke from the old men's pipes, almost feel the excitement of two young girls cawing across the tundra, like gulls, wanting to be first to spread the news: They come! They come! The Siberians have come!

Book I
Nutaaq's Story
1917

Iġñivik—in the-time-of-birth

The Trade Fair at Sheshalik

The Siberians are traveling with us to the trade fair, traveling along the coast, their boats piled high with the reindeer skins they have brought to trade. Our dogs run along the shore like shadows, their packs bouncing against their ribs—happy to be out in the late night sun, happy to be free. I am happy, too, gliding along in our skin boat, watching them run, wishing I could stretch my limbs and run with them, run for the sheer joy of it, as they do.

How glorious it is when summer comes again! Glorious to be out on the open water of the summer sea in the night-long sun, watching the bright ocean ice drift by, dreamlike, on the smooth dark water. Watching the grassy tundra roll past us, nearly close enough to touch, thick with the smell of sunshine and earth and greenery—*Aarigaa!*

Newborn animals are everywhere, too—birds and caribou and even baby seals—and we ourselves are soon to have a newborn of our own. Nuna, traveling with us, is round as a whale and clumsy in her unaccustomed shape, always forgetting she can no longer bend as fast as a child, and often impatient for her time to come.

Because it's her first, Mama said one time.

Because it's a girl, a big round girl, Aaka had countered, clicking her tongue and frowning the way grandmothers do sometimes. *We need another hunter in this family!*

Tupaaq smiled wide, eyeing Aaluk: *Girls can be good hunters, too*, he said, winking at me. *Girls are good with arrows.*

Tupaaq had asked Aaluk to ride in his boat that time, but Aaluk said no, muttering to herself how she'd rather run with the dogs. Aaka had frowned at this, because Tupaaq is from Aaka's village, the village of my father's people, and Aaka favors him.

I'll go, I said. *I'll go in Tupaaq's boat.*

But Mama shook her head.

You're too little, she said.

Too little for what? I had wondered, tall as I was. I was big, nearly bigger than Aaluk—big enough, certainly, to ride in Tupaaq's well-made boat.

I'm big enough, I said. Saying it just like that, too, as bossy as Aaluk.

Big like a lemming. Aaluk laughed. Tupaaq laughed, too, which made my cheeks grow warm.

Wait until you grow bigger, little lemming. Just wait, Tupaaq said. Which made me feel like the lemming in the story Tupaaq always tells, the one stuck underneath an old sealskin, hollering at the top of his lungs.

Suddenly, I want to holler, too, sitting here in my father's boat. I had waited so long for this trip to begin, but now, I realize, I'm ready for it to end, for the excitement of the trade fair to start. Waiting to hear the sound of the drums welcoming us into the Sheshalik inlet and waiting to hear the wavering note of the women's voices, clear as water, singing the songs of Sheshalik, the Sheshalik welcoming songs.

WE BEGIN TO HEAR their songs when we are still too far away to even see the people. The drums—we hear the drums first. The sound grows louder and louder, pulling us swiftly across the surface of the water, guiding us toward the spit of land, green with summer, that is Sheshalik.

As we round the final bend, the drumming begins to throb in the air around us like a heartbeat and the sweet shrillness of the women's voices shoots across the surface of the water in bright arrows of sound.

Baby Manu, bouncing on her mother's back in the front of our boat, squeals with delight, trying to sing as the women sing. I, too, am barely able to keep myself from squealing along with her.

My father has raised our flag, the flag of our whalers, and as soon as the drummers see it, their song changes and they begin, at once, to drum one of our own songs, announcing our arrival with our own music. Suddenly I feel very proud to be from the island, proud to claim such a brave song as the song of my own people, hearing it as if with new ears. The drumming grows louder and louder as we approach the shore, and soon the sound of our own voices joins with the sounds of theirs, sweet as birdsong.

Welcoming.

Sheshalik, at first sight, is too big to believe—all the tents, the caribou-skin tents of our people, stretching out along the edge of the beach and reaching up inland as far as the eye can see. Overflowing with the sounds of happiness—the kind of happiness that only comes of many, many people, all coming together as one.

This is my first impression of the Sheshalik trade fair, that all the people of the world must be here. Everyone in the entire world, all here at Sheshalik, preparing to trade.

People have indeed come from many distant places, each group bringing the specialties of its own region. We ourselves have sealskin pokes full of seal oil, and split walrus skins for boat-making, because our women are the most skillful at preparing these. We also have coils and coils of sealskin rope, strong enough to pull a whale. The rope our men make is always in high demand by those from other regions. We will trade these island things for stone from the People-of-the-Land, soapstone and jade from the mountains up inland, the kind used for lamps, seal-oil lamps.

Aaluk will, of course, need a lamp of her own, now that she has become a woman. A pretty new lamp carved of jade, perhaps, or a smooth one of polished soapstone. A lamp to heat her own home, when she leaves ours for the home of her husband, whoever he may be. But not me. I have no use for a lamp just yet. Nor for a husband.

I've been eyeing the Siberian reindeer skins for the length of our trip together—white as snow and supple as water, piled high in the Siberians' boats. I am wanting a new parka, a pretty new parka of Siberian reindeer, soft and light and easy to run in. I would have it with a dark wolverine ruff and leather trim dyed red with willow bark, the way the inland people make it. I hope Papa will trade one of our seal-oil pokes for enough skins for a new parka for me.

It doesn't take long to unpack our gear, and soon our tent

is snug as home with thick skins on the floor and new people crowding in to greet us. We offer them dried seal meat, soaked in oil, my mother's specialty. The meat is moist and chewy, rich with the flavor of the oil. The men are eating it in great quantities, telling stories and making jokes and singing little snatches of their songs. They are all smoking Siberian tobacco, too, and we sit watching the way the smoke from their pipes curls up toward the open nose of our tent in skinny little trails. As I watch, the strands of sweet-smelling smoke wind round and round one another, dissolving up through the tent's nose and out into the open sky.

The smoke makes our eyes water and tickles our noses, making Baby Manu sneeze and sneeze, laughing every time. All of us children are laughing—sneezing and laughing, sneezing and laughing, until pretty soon none of us can tell which is which. So very good it is, to laugh together with all the many, many peoples who have come to Sheshalik to trade.

My sister, Aaluk, is not laughing at all, however. Aaluk, who is usually the center of everything, sits apart from the rest of us children—neither sneezing nor laughing. Acting as if she is already far too old for such silliness, when in truth she is but a few winters older than I. She makes a very pretty picture, however, sitting there so neat and composed, her dark hair smooth as a still river, her new tattoo as delicate as a flower's stem.

In truth, I am a bit jealous of her, because it seems to me she is everything I'm not. I have not yet been marked by womanhood—my face is smudged with dust alone. My hair, too, flies in every direction, like tundra grass, and I am much too distracted to sit still and pretty the way Aaluk does.

Watching her eat her soup, her hands moving like graceful brown birds, I suddenly feel clumsy.

That one Siberian is watching her, too. The one who wears a string of large blue beads. His dark eyes follow Aaluk the way a wolf watches a caribou, never resting. I do not know this man and his bold stare scares me. Is he good or is he evil? And Aaluk is watching him as well, watching shyly, her eyes down—Aaluk who has never in her life been shy about anything. Aaluk, the bossy one, who has always turned her chin to the boys. Boys, Aaluk says, are rough and blustering and not worth the bother.

But now here she is, watching that Siberian—who after all is only an older boy—watching him the way he watches her: neither of them laughing, barely even blinking or smiling, their eyes full of sparks. That boy-man, who has placed his sealskin parka next to my father's and now sits on my mother's skins, his beads glowing blue against his broad brown chest.

I am immediately drawn to those beads. They are so blue, so very blue that I want, desperately, to touch them, to touch one of them, just once. But, of course, I do not.

You can barely imagine a blue of such power, glowing in the lamplight as if lit by an internal magic. Blue the way certain fish are blue in shallow water, their scales flashing blue in the sunlight—a blue like that, only different. A kind of blue none of us have ever seen before. It feels strange to me and a little frightening, the power of those beads and of the man wearing them.

I look away, determined to be bothered no more by all of this.

Baby Manu is toddling toward me with a serious look on

her little face. I reach out my arms and she tries to move faster, but instead topples down with a plop. Her mouth starts to pout and I know she is about to cry, but she looks like such a funny little fish that I cannot help but laugh. When she sees me laughing, she stops pouting and smiles, too, looking at me with trusting eyes as if to say: If you think it's funny, it must be so. I reach out again, asking her with my own eyes if she wants to come to me. *Yes?* I ask, raising my eyebrows. She looks up at me, lifting her own eyebrows to say yes, too, just like a big person.

I scoop her up into my arms and she nuzzles her head under my chin and begins sucking her thumb, falling asleep at once. We lean back together against a pile of skins, and let the old men's stories wash over us in waves of sound that rise and fall with emotion, making people laugh with delight in one moment and gasp in terror the next.

Old Stories

Everyone at Sheshalik has stories, even the Siberians. And their stories, as it turns out, are much like ours. The Siberians tell their stories and we tell ours and after a while the words begin to weave themselves together into one story. *Our story*, the story of our people.

My uncle Saġġan tells about the trail that used to go all the way to Siberia, back in the days before our village became an island, lifting its head from the sea like a seal. Back in those days, our home was a mountain, its cliffs rising above the clouds. We lived on the spine of land that bridged our world to the Siberian world. Way back then, before the earth turned over and the bridge of land was torn in two. We didn't need sealskin boats for visiting back then, didn't need to strain our eyes seaward, watching. All we needed were feet for running. Fast. How I would have loved to run across that trail in those days, dancing along on outstretched legs, faster than even the fastest of dogs, for I am a runner and I could have done it!

Uncle Saġġan is telling, too, about how, when the earth was cracking apart, one girl played the game we call Mauraġaraġaq there, right at the crack, jumping back and forth across it, playing the game even as the earth was moving, just as we play it today on pieces of moving ocean ice. Trying to take one last leap without plunging into the rift.

Her name was Iñuuraq, that girl.

Tupaaq, of course, tells his lemming story, which is mostly for kids. And the way he tells it grabs the kids' attention right away, too.

Once there was a young boy who had gone camping up the coast, all alone, far from his village.

Tupaaq's voice is hushed and all the kids sit up straight, trying to hear him. The ones who know the story are already smiling.

So here he is, all alone in his tent preparing to sleep, when suddenly he hears the sound of a voice whispering in the darkness.

Tupaaq pauses for effect.

"I am big!" Tupaaq whispers, *"as big as the world!" This is what the voice is saying, and, of course, the boy, who was almost asleep, sits up quickly, suddenly scared. Who is it?*

Tupaaq pauses again. The smallest kids fidget with fear.

And then the voice comes again, this time closer, Tupaaq whispers, straightening up like a bear, searching.

"My feet dig deep beneath the sand! My head touches the top of the sky! I am big!"

Tupaaq's voice is pounding now. He leans down slowly and looks right into the eyes of the smallest child.

Who is this giant?

Tupaaq becomes a giant himself, filling the room with his story.

"*I AM BIG, BIG, BIG. COME SEE ME IF YOU DARE,*" Tupaaq roars suddenly.

Some of the kids squeal with delight while others fly to their mothers' laps in terror.

Ah, but this is a very brave boy, Tupaaq says. *And he is not about to sit in his tent, waiting for his fate. He grabs his knife and steps outside, prepared to meet the owner of that voice. He follows the sound of it up the beach:* BIG. BIG. BIG. *Closer and closer until finally . . .*

It's only a lemming! one of the older boys shouts suddenly.

Yes, says Tupaaq, laughing. *It's only a lemming. Only a little bitty lemming no bigger than your fist, stuck underneath a piece of sealskin. And he thinks he's really big, because he has convinced himself that the bottom of that skin is the top of the sky!*

Everyone laughs along with Tupaaq, even the babies, and I smile, too, thinking about what a good storyteller Tupaaq is and imagining myself retelling this same story someday to my own children. Showing them how foolish it is to brag. Perhaps I will even tell it to my grandchildren one day.

Who knows?

Uqaluktuaq

New Stories

There are lots of other stories at Sheshalik, some old, like
Tupaaq's story, but some about recent events, too, like
the stories about Maniilaq, which people are telling over and
over from one tent to the next. Maniilaq was a prophet who
told of things to come. He even predicted the coming of the
boot-sole people, the ones with faces the color of bleached
sealskin, the kind used for boot soles. Maniilaq said these
people would come, but he died long before they actually did
come, so how could he have known? This is what I wonder.

The one called Uyaġak is speaking of this right now and
so many people have crowded into our tent to hear his
words that it is hard to find space to even breathe.

Uyaġak, *the rock:* his words are as hard as his name.

*If a shaman should cut a hole in someone's parka, what will
happen?*

No one answers because everyone knows. If a shaman
does such a thing, the person wearing the parka will die.

What must one do to protect oneself?

Repair the tear, someone says.

No! Uyaġak cries triumphantly, as though he had been waiting for exactly this answer. *It is not enough to repair a single tear. A new way has come with the new people, just as Maniilaq has foreseen it, and those following it will be forever protected. Those who fail to follow will die in the cold as if with parkas full of holes.*

Uyaġak is staring intently at Nuna, big and round with her baby. Nuna shifts uncomfortably.

It is said we must banish a woman to a lonely sod hut when her time is come. Why? Is she evil? Do we do this simply because the shaman has said so? Uyaġak asks.

Some people are nodding their heads, and glancing at one another nervously. Nuna blushes and looks away.

In the days to come, we will no longer fear the shaman. In the days to come, huge boats, powered by fire, will fly through the sky and a new people will cover the land, bringing the Word, as Maniilaq first heard it in his vision. This is true, as you yourselves can see: it is already happening. The new ones have already come.

An old man spits loudly and lights his pipe.

Uyaġak jumps up, suddenly pointing at the group of girls I sit with. We all squirm. It is not good to point at people in this way.

You, he says, *will follow the new way.*

He moves closer, singling out two of the youngest among us.

Your babies and yours will be born into the new way.

Now some of the old men are laughing heartily and we ourselves have even begun to giggle, hiding our mouths with our hands. The girls he points at are hardly bigger than babies themselves and we can't imagine them having babies of their own.

But our laughter seems to fuel Uyaġak's fervor. He jumps into the middle of the room suddenly, holding out a strange kind of amulet in a way that frightens us into silence.

This has the power to vanquish the shaman's evil! he cries.

Some of the old men continue to chuckle, as though Uyaġak's outburst is all part of a good show. But most of the others look around with frightened eyes, because even though there is no shaman here in this tent, everyone understands that it is bad to speak in this way of the shaman, very bad to ignore the laws of our people.

The shaman's way is an evil way, Uyaġak says.

Nonsense, Uncle mutters.

I look from Uncle to Uyaġak, uncertain of what to think. There are bad shamans, to be sure, but there are also good ones, like the kind one from our village who heals people's ailments with gentle hands. How can these be called evil?

Maybe shamans are just people, some good, some bad, just like everyone else. Just people. That's what I'm thinking. I don't speak this aloud, of course. Listening to Uyaġak talk of all the things we are warned not to talk of has scared me so much that I have nearly ceased breathing. Surely something bad will come of talk such as this.

Then I look at my sister, Aaluk, and I see that she is not frightened, not at all. My sister, Aaluk, is watching Uyaġak with a new light in her eyes, and I can see that she believes everything she is hearing and she likes it, too, likes it very much. My sister, who is no longer afraid of the shaman, smiling softly at Uyaġak's rock-hard words.

The Siberian is smiling, too, but he is not smiling at

Uyaġak's words, I don't think. He is smiling at my sister, smiling as if he will believe whatever she believes, just to see her smile that way.

But I'm not so sure. Listening to Uyaġak, it feels as though I am being asked to decide against our old ways in favor of the new. And why should I have to decide, anyhow? There are so many people here—a whole world full of happy people, telling stories and singing songs and laughing. Who needs to consider rock-hard questions when there are so many reasons to be happy?

I am not at all disappointed when Uyaġak moves on to another tent.

I FALL ASLEEP listening to one of the Sheshalik men telling a story. It's a story about a young girl who is claimed by a shaman and is flown directly to the shaman's *iglu*, pulled headlong through the frozen night sky by a force she can't resist.

In my sleep I am the one flying high above the ocean ice, hurtling helplessly through gales of snow, dashed like a sled through the *kiuġuya*, the deadly dancing lights of the *kiuġuya*. I feel my hair flying against my cheeks and realize suddenly that I am not wearing my parka hood.

Iiqinii!

Suddenly I am frozen with fear because the northern lights, it is said, are angry spirits who play ball games with people's heads—especially the heads of young people foolish enough to walk beneath them without putting their hoods on.

Where is Aaluk? I wonder suddenly. Where is my sister? Did she, too, get taken by a shaman? Yes, she did. I am certain of it, certain that the *kiuġuya* are, at this very moment, playing football with my sister's head.

Aaluk, Aaluk!

Even as I call her name, I feel the sleeping skins beneath me and realize, of course, that I am still secure in the warmth of our tent, still surrounded by the smell of good food and the sound of laughter, feeling only the hand of my sister, Aaluk, touching my shoulder.

What were you dreaming of, little lemming? Aaluk asks.

I wouldn't want to fly through the sky trapped by a shaman, I whisper. *I would be frightened.*

I wouldn't be frightened, my sister assures me, smiling her beautiful, believing smile. *I wouldn't be frightened at all.*

But she is not smiling at me—I see this at once. She is smiling boldly at the Siberian with his blue, blue beads. And he is smiling back.

I wouldn't be afraid of flying through the sky like a bird, Aaluk says. *And I would fly, at once, in the boat powered by fire, which Maniilaq has said will come.*

Aaluk's voice is light with laughter, watching the Siberian, her fingers picking daintily at our mother's *mikigaq*. But my sister's eyes do not smile. They are as sharp as an owl's, hunting.

I wouldn't be scared at all, my sister says.

Especially not in a Siberian-made boat, one of the old men says with a chuckle. And everyone else laughs, too, even Papa, laughing his deep drum of a laugh.

Everyone is laughing but me. Me and Tupaaq, Tupaaq who would have let my sister travel forever in *his* well-made boat, had she only let him.

Games

They play games at Sheshalik, too, many, many games: the high kick, the stick pull, the seal hop, footraces, ball games, and boat races. Not only do the different villages compete with one another—the Alaskans compete with the Siberians as well. Back home in our village, Tupaaq is the one who always wins. But the Siberian with his dark flashing eyes is good at games, too, and he kicks higher than anyone else, even Tupaaq. Tupaaq beats him at the stick pull, though, because Tupaaq is stronger.

Now they are competing in the seal hop and I am very glad I do not have to compete in this event, because the seal hop is a test of endurance. I would not want to endure hopping along the rocky beach letting nothing touch the ground but my toes and tender knuckles.

The two of them—Tupaaq and the Siberian—are stretched out horizontal, facedown, holding themselves up by the tips of their toes and the edges of their knuckles, their fists clenched. This is painful, even just to watch, and suddenly I am very worried. Tupaaq is much heavier than the Siberian, so the pain to his knuckles will be far greater. How can he possibly win? He is trying, of course, to make it look as if he feels nothing, springing alongside the Siberian, his face muscles bulging. He is trying his best to smile, I know, but his smile seems more of a grimace. The Siberian, on the other hand, looks as if he is truly enjoying himself. He hops rapidly across the beach, his knuckles plunging into the sharp rocky sand as if into bird feathers. The muscles along his back and arms ripple like tundra grass in the wind and his deep blue beads swing from side to side as he moves. All the young women are watching him intently, whispering about how strong and handsome he is. Wondering about his wealth.

One of those blue beads is worth much, it is said: a boat and a dog team, perhaps even a sled as well. We all stare at those beads—especially my sister—watching the way they dangle from his dark neck, bouncing from side to side as he moves, as if daring us to grab them.

The Siberian finishes long before Tupaaq and stands before us smiling triumphantly at my sister, who tries, unsuccessfully, to act shy and disinterested.

Now it is time for footraces and I am certain the Siberian will beat Tupaaq at this one as well, because Tupaaq is not a natural runner. Tupaaq excels at games of strength, not games of speed. I watch him, worried. I cannot bear to see him lose again to this arrogant Siberian. We are told that it is wrong to brag, wrong to boast of one's abilities, and yet every move this man makes seems a kind of boastfulness. Now he stands at the edge of the beach, calling for the runners from all the villages, standing there as if certain of the outcome, daring the others to compete. I glance nervously at Tupaaq, standing next to me. Does he feel, already, the humiliation of yet another defeat? But Tupaaq is watching me, a huge smile spreading across his strong, dark face.

Run against him, little lemming, Tupaaq whispers. *You're faster than any of those men. Go show them.*

His words make my heart beat hard with pride. And he's right, too: I am fast. I am smaller and lighter but my legs are long, longer than a grown man's. Everyone from our village knows that I am our fastest runner, even if I am only a young girl. They all look at me, nodding happily. Even little Manu, who cannot possibly understand about races, nods with the rest. They all want me to run.

The race will take us from the edge of the beach to a spot some distance up inland, a place by the lake where the people of Sheshalik get water. Every village sponsors their fastest runner, but I am the only girl.

The Siberian opens the round of races with a challenge to one of the villages east of us. We will continue running, one village against another, until one of us has beaten all the others.

The Siberian takes the first race, his legs long and lean and muscular, like mine. I watch as he quickly outstrips his competition with wide easy strides. He looks, as he runs, the way I imagine I must look—comfortable and content, as if running, for him, is akin to breathing. I pull my hair back and wrap it tighter, hopping lightly from one foot to the other, full of nervous energy.

One after another, I outrun the racers from the other villages, watching as the Siberian does the same.

At long last we have beaten all of our other competitors, the Siberian and I, and now we are ready for the final race—the one that will decide which village wins all. Suddenly I realize it's more than a race between villages. It has become a race between the Siberians and the Alaskans. I suck in great gulps of cool air, wondering if I am really capable of outrunning this strong dark man. The Siberian looks at me and smiles. It's a sharp smile, full of teeth and not at all warm, the way Tupaaq's smile is warm. It's a smile I don't even care to look at, so I look instead at those beads—those blue, blue beads that hang heavily from his neck. And suddenly I am torn by the strangest desire. More than anything else, I want to reach out and rip those beads right off his hard, muscled neck. They seem to demand a respect that, to my mind, he's yet to earn. And I don't like the way my sister is always watching him, drawn, as I am, by the power of those beads.

His eyes follow mine and, as if he can hear my thoughts, he removes the beads from his neck and hands them to me. They are heavy and warm in my hand, alive with a magic so strong it makes my fingers tingle.

I catch my breath.

These are the kind of beads used to calm the spirits that bring sickness and death, the kind one puts in a grave to fool death. I can feel their power.

If you beat me, I will give them to your sister, the Siberian says, nodding at his beads, his smile mocking.

Part of me wants to cry, *No! Give them to me!* But, of course, I don't. And when he takes those beads and hangs them around Aaluk's neck, I am happy I've kept my mouth shut, for the beads look as though they belong there, resting brightly against Aaluk's rosy-brown skin. As though they were specially made to complement her long dark hair and her new tattoo. And she is no longer watching the Siberian, either. My sister, Aaluk, gazes out to sea instead, as though she sees something wonderful out there, something completely beyond our deepest dreams.

Do you ever wonder? her eyes seem to say. *Do you ever wonder about that glittering world hovering out there beyond the edge of the sky?*

All of a sudden I want to win this race so badly I can barely stop my feet from racing off toward the lake. All of a sudden I am quite certain I can beat this Siberian man. And claim his beads for my sister and me. Claim them for our village.

I am ready.

Kik! Kik! The people have begun to holler, impatient for us to start. Anxious to know the outcome of the final race. *Kik!*

We take off side by side, our strides nearly matched. The sun is bright and the air is deliciously cool and one can smell, clear and distinct, the odor of sea ice. As we leave the tents behind and begin moving inland, the sound of birdsong rings shrill and sweet across the tundra and I am not even aware, anymore, of the Siberian. I am taking joy in the running itself. Sheer joy.

When I finally glance southward, I see that he is running beside me, at a distance, like a dark shadow. Like the shadow of a bird moving swiftly across the tundra, his running is even with my own. Our limbs move parallel to one another in a way that makes me feel as though we are connected

somehow. As though I am a bird and he is my shadow, gliding across the land.

I am the bird and he is the shadow. I say it over and over to
myself as I run: *I am the bird and he is the shadow.*

We can see the lake now, glittering against the tundra like
a dark bead, and I want, more than anything else, to reach
out and touch it, running my fingers along its smooth surface, flying ahead of the Siberian. But to do so I must break
this easy bond that has formed between us. To beat him, I
must break even my own rhythm and pull ahead. But it feels,
suddenly, as if there is no way I can possibly do this. The
Siberian holds me into the rhythm of our running with a grip
as hard as shorefast ice. My breathing begins to feel flat and
knifelike against my breast as I strain to break it.

I will myself to ignore the pain, thinking only of those
blue beads, the power of those blue, blue beads. I can still
feel the warmth of them tingling against my hand. I clench
my fist and run harder, finally moving out ahead of the
Siberian.

The beads will be ours.

All of a sudden I see myself leaping across the finish line
ahead of me, all the people cheering, and I know, with certainty, I've already won. This knowledge lends a sudden
burst of energy to my legs and propels me forward. Faster
than a bird I fly, dropping the Siberian shadow behind me
like a discarded parka.

The beads are mine. The beads are already ours.

I can see the people waiting for us by the edge of the lake,
and can see, clearly, the faces of my own people, triumphant,
watching me pull ahead of the Siberian. And I can hear their
voices, too, growing closer and closer.

Kik! Kik! they holler, like a flock of insistent birds: *KIK! NUTAAQ! KIK!* My people know I can do it, have already done it. I have only the feather of a lead over the Siberian, but it is enough. I can feel the finish now and I know, without a doubt, it is enough.

Suddenly there is a snap of pain in my ankle and a crack of darkness and I am staring up at the clouds wheeling across the sky, watching the Siberian leap past me to the finish. I bite my cheek to keep from wailing. I have tripped over a hummock and the Siberian has secured the finish with a single stride. One single stride. I have lost the beads.

My sister, Aaluk, races to my side.

Is it broken? Is your ankle broken?

No, the pain was only a brief stab and now the only thing left hurting is my pride. The Siberian reaches down and offers his hand, and I am bound, out of courtesy, to take it.

I stand between them—the Siberian and my sister—looking at those beads, those beads that were supposed to be ours. That's when I hear the words—the words our elders say to hunters: *Never catch an animal before you've caught it.*

That's what I've done. I had won those beads in my mind before I'd actually won the race. I look at the Siberian, wanting to be furious with him, but angry only at myself for my own foolishness. I am as foolish as a silly lemming.

I look again at my sister, blinking back my tears.

The Siberian reaches over and I imagine him pulling those beads from her neck, but instead he touches them. He touches just one of the beads, touches it very gently with just one finger.

This is where these beads belong, he says.

And suddenly I want to cry out loudly: *No! Take them*

away! Take them back to Siberia! Cross the far horizon and toss them into the sea! But when I see my sister's face, my sister's beautiful, smiling, believing face, I, of course, remain silent.

I feel tricked, tricked as though life itself has tricked me and there is nothing I can do about it. Nothing at all.

*Amiġaiqsivik—in the-time-when-the-caribou-
antlers-shed-their-velvet*

The Village of My Mother's People

Manu is no longer the baby of our group. Nuna's baby was born at Sheshalik—a boy after all, a big round boy with feathery black hair and dark, serious eyes. He was born the way Uyaġak said, right in our own tent and without any difficulties. Uyaġak himself blessed him, using words from a thing the boot-sole people call a Bi-ble, words spoken in our own language. They were strong words, too, the way Uyaġak said them, and Nuna is happy.

But I am not at all happy, because right now, as we leave Sheshalik for my mother's village, my sister rides in the Siberian's boat instead of ours. And later, when the Siberians leave us, she will go with them. They were married by Uyaġak at Sheshalik, married in front of everyone in a way different from the old way, a way that seemed very strange.

I don't want my sister to sail out past the last bend just as the winter snow is about to fly. I don't want her to go at all, not even if it is to a land full of purple mountains and blue,

blue beads and black tea thick with sugar. But Nuna's baby is so sweet and warm on my own back, where Nuna has allowed me to carry him, that it's really hard to feel sad for any length of time. And little Manu, sitting in front of us like a big girl, smiles and coos back at us.

Manu is trying to talk now. She calls *Aahaa! Aahaa!* every time she sees a flock of ducks flying. She's trying to say *aahaaliq*, of course, for ducks are flying in thick flocks these days. Manu calls everything that flies *aahaa*, even the geese, which makes us all smile and makes Papa laugh his deep rolling laugh. And when Papa laughs, Manu laughs, too, a little baby laugh that sounds like the call of some new kind of bird, a fat, happy little bird.

The way Manu laughs, always smiling, makes me want to hug and hug her until I forget all about Aaluk's leaving. How can anyone be unhappy when the air is so full of sunshine and baby sounds?

BEFORE WE EVEN have time to grow weary of our travel, we arrive at Kingigin, the village of my mother's people—our boat, the Siberian's boat, and Tupaaq's boat, where Aaka sits, wrapped in furs, her eyes closed. All at once our aunties begin fussing over us and our uncles begin making jokes to us about boys, especially Siberian boys. And the Siberians beam, especially my sister's Siberian. My auntie Ubliuk admires the many reindeer skins the Siberian has given my father, eyeing them carefully and looking to me as though fitting them perfectly with her seamstress eyes. Now that I am nearly a woman like my sister, I must have a new parka, Ubliuk says. She and I will make it together, she tells me, and we will trim it in red, too, just as I imagined. I will be the prettiest girl around—just as pretty as my very pretty sister, Auntie Ubliuk says.

I don't tell Ubliuk I would rather run with the boys herding reindeer than sit inside sewing skins, even very fine skins such as these. Nor do I worry much about being pretty—of what use is it to be pretty? But I know better than to speak rudely to my auntie. And the way she describes it, my new parka will be well worth the sitting.

We are to spend the season here at Kingigin, helping with the harvest of the Kingigin reindeer. It will be fun, but I can't help looking out to sea, toward our little island and beyond, dreading the day my sister will cross that horizon.

Once we have settled in, Aaluk begins preparing for her trip by sewing the new clothes she will need. Now that she is married, her stitches have become as neat as Auntie's. Aaluk, of course, has always had a gift for sewing, not like me.

My stitches are like a mess of fish bones and Auntie makes me rip them out and resew them again and again. Truly, I am not much of a seamstress.

No, not that way, Auntie keeps saying. Saying it so often that my ears begin to burn with the sound.

Even when my stitches are straight, the seams refuse to lie flat. Even my very best stitches somehow make the seams pucker and gather. Instead of forming a straight line, as they ought to, my seams weave back and forth like rivers. And every time Auntie restarts a seam, I want to run outside and scream into the wind, running faster than the sound of my own voice.

You need to learn patience, says Aaluk, raising her chin in a way that makes me want to rip the seams out of that word, *patience*.

When you sew for your husband, Aaka says, *the seams must be tight and straight. A hunter cannot be successful in a parka full of holes and puckers.*

I suppress an urge to wrinkle my nose and spit. Of what use is a husband if having one forces one to sit inside and sew tedious seams while the tundra turns golden red and the last lingering light just begs for someone to go out and enjoy it? I sigh, turning my attention back to my stitches, taking great care to make each one perfect, trying my best to keep the seam flat. I grit my teeth with concentration. My parka will not be full of holes and it will not pucker at the sides. My parka will be perfect. Just as perfect as Aaluk's.

Leaving

Today, the first snow is falling. I am not at all sad to see it because snow means the reindeer are getting fat, readying themselves for winter. Already the enticing aroma of rich reindeer soup fills my auntie's house, making my mouth water.

Soon the fall storms will come. My father says we are to spend the winter here, herding reindeer for my uncle to replenish our own supplies of meat. I, of course, would rather go home to our own island because I miss the sound of the waves slapping against the rocks. Here, there is nothing but sand and grass, so the waves merely hiss.

The Siberians are preparing to leave today, taking Aaluk with them, going away before the storms set in. Aaluk sits with me, saying nothing, braiding my hair. Her fingers linger, slow, smoothing my hair into a long black rope, her hands saying what our mouths cannot.

There, she says finally, running her fingers across my braid.

We sit quietly, too full of hard thoughts to speak. Then she pulls me aside, slightly, and presses two small things into my hand like two hard round secrets.

You look like a grown woman, Nutaaq. Soon you, too, will take a husband, she says loudly, touching my hand gently and warning me with her eyes to say nothing.

I know, without looking, that she has given me two of her precious beads.

For you and me—the two of us, she whispers. *One for Aaluk and one for Nutaaq. When I come home, I will bring you a whole string of them. One bead for everyone in our family.*

I am still clutching the beads—two big blue beads, tingling with magic—when we go down to the beach to watch the Siberians leave. I think of Aaluk's promise: one bead for everyone in our family; and as the boys shove the boats off, I force myself to stand firm, ticking off our family names in my head, biting back the pain. *Aaluk. Mama, Papa, Aaka, Ubliuk, Nagazruk, Jukku, Amaġuq, Ayałhuq, Manu, Nuna . . .*

I lean into Mama and hold my breath to keep from crying as my sister's boat pulls away from the sandy shore.

It's all right, Nutaaq, Mama whispers. *We'll see her again come summer.*

But it doesn't feel that way to me. It doesn't feel that way at all. Watching the Siberian boats leave, tightly packed for the ocean crossing, it feels to me as though they will never return, as though they will cross the distant horizon and disappear forever into a world as purple as a new bruise.

I clutch the beads hard to keep from crying as we wave

goodbye, clutch them hard enough to hurt the bones of my hand. I don't want a whole string of blue beads. I want my sister. I want to pull her beneath a sealskin blanket and hide her from the Siberians. I want my sister, Aaluk, to stay home. With me.

But she is gone now—no more than a speck of light on the edge of the horizon. Vanished into the hazy purple sun.

Inland

My new parka is finished at last and I am glad because my cousin Nagazruk has invited me to go up inland to reindeer camp. Now Auntie no longer has an excuse to keep me inside.

I stand there, before my mother, my aunt, my *aaka*, and all the other women, wearing my parka, turning round and round so all can see the fine work of the trim, which makes a pretty pattern along the hem with different shades of fur. Auntie has matched the different skins in the body of the parka, matched them in such a way that the fur itself makes a beautiful pattern. It is light and warm and fits perfectly and I am suddenly aware of the fact that I am no longer a little girl. I've changed since we left the island. I'm not sure exactly how, but I can feel it like a small secret knotted up inside. Soon, I think, I, too, will wear the tattoo of a woman.

Suddenly I am not at all sure how I feel about this. I'm excited, of course, but also a little frightened. I think of that

Siberian who stole my sister and I am struck with a sudden urge to race outdoors and forget all about new parkas and tattoos and strange Siberian men.

You are a pretty flower, Auntie says, beaming. *You will make a beautiful bride.*

My father laughs. *Stop teasing her, Ubliuk. Let her be my baby a bit longer. Maybe next year, we might talk of marriage, but not today. Today she is still her papa's little girl.*

I listen to my father's laughter, reassured. I am my papa's baby yet. I will get to run out on the tundra with the boys one last season, at least.

Little Manu stands at my feet, pulling at my new parka, saying *up* with her eyes. Little Manu thinks I am grown enough to be her mother. I pick her up and twirl her around, wishing I could take her to reindeer camp with me.

You are too little, I tell her. *You still need your Mama's milk.*

Then, as though she understands my words, she sticks her little thumb in her mouth and begins to suck.

I LOVE the smell of autumn on the tundra, love the colors, gold and russet. Love running the distance, the long cool distance to the herder's camp, with my cousins.

The deer fill an entire valley up inland, all bunched together like a huge litter of puppies, eating tundra grass. When I first see them, they look like grass themselves, like a thick brown blanket of grass, covering the ruddy earth. When they move, they move in waves, so it looks as if the earth itself is moving.

As I get closer, I see a tangle of horns and heads and dark liquid eyes.

They look very much like their cousins, the caribou, only

the caribou have different-looking heads and move faster. Nagazruk's reindeer came from Siberia some years ago, my mother told us, brought over in huge ships and given to the people of my mother's village so we might have herds of our own to feed ourselves and to feed the boot-sole people who come, just as Maniilaq predicted, in ever-increasing numbers.

The boys have their tent set on a hill at the edge of the herd and we sit together in the dwindling sunshine, drinking tea with sugar and eating crackers, just like rich people. My uncle keeps his boys very well supplied, taking good care of them so that they, in turn, will take good care of the deer. Outside the tent, they have a meat cache made of driftwood poles, with a high shelf to keep the meat protected from prowling bear and fox and wolverine. The corner poles tower high above the rack, tied on the ends with bones that rattle in the wind to scare off the birds.

What kind of bones are they? I ask.

Polar bear, Nagazruk says.

Polar bear bones will keep even the wolves away— wolves and bad spirits. That's what my cousins tell me. My cousins who herd reindeer. There are three of them: Nagazruk, Amaġuq, and Jukku, who likes to tease and tell stories.

They are all runners, my cousins, runners nearly as fast as me, running to and from the camp for supplies and running around the herd to keep strays from wandering. Running is a good skill for a herder. Nagazruk runs so fast he can catch a stray deer in just a few quick strides, but mostly he doesn't have to. Mostly his deer will listen to him, almost as dogs listen, flicking their ears when he whistles, then turning, as a herd, to follow his call.

Because they are curious, Nagazruk says. Curious about the strange sound of the whistle, I think.

The boys have to watch the deer carefully because sometimes the caribou come too close and try to lure them away into the wild. It is better for them to stay here, protected from the wolves. They don't know the country as the caribou do and they aren't as fast. It's safer for them to remain in one place, close to us, eating grass and lichen.

AT NIGHT, when I step outside the tent with a warm cup of soup, the lights of the reindeers' eyes twinkle in the dark valley below, like an earthbound constellation, and the stars above seem to blink back, as though in greeting. It's peaceful here and I feel light as a bird, skimming across the surface of things. The only sound in the stillness of this night is the occasional mooing of a lone deer, complaining, and the occasional laughter of my cousins inside the tent, telling stories. The soup in my stomach is rich and warm, and life is right.

I even welcome the sudden singing of the wolves, far off in the mountains. They howl in long drawn-out trails of wavering sound, and as I stand outside listening, I think I can almost recognize the words in their voices—eerie, mournful words. I step back inside the tent, shivering, but Nagazruk remains outside, watching. The wolves are getting closer, he says. Someone must remain on watch.

Inside the tent, my cousins are drinking hot tea, syrupy with sugar, and telling scary stories. They sit bunched up close together like a small herd of boys, their eyes wide.

Whales used to fly, my cousin Jukku says. *They used to swoop down from the sky and capture large animals, the way an owl grabs a lemming.*

This is true; we know it for a fact. Back in the old days, the big gentle whales called *aġviq* used to fly like massive birds of prey and the smaller ones with the fierce black fins used to roam the land in packs like wolves. These two kinds existed before the whales and wolves, as we know them today, came into being. And the ones that flew used to eat the ones that walked the earth. This is how it was.

Jukku makes his eyes grow big. *You can hear them,* he whispers, *flapping down from the mountains, their wings as black as death, their numbers drowning out the moon and stars. The sky is screaming with the sound of their wings, and people run to hide, but there is no place to hide.* Jukku holds his ears, as if in great pain. *Zzzzz-zzzz—zzzz. And today, even the wolves remember the sound of the flying whales, and when they hear that sound again, they run away in terror.*

Jukku pulls a wolf-scare out of his pocket. It is made of baleen from the mouth of the whale—a flat oval disk, carved round with notches. And when you swing it hard, by its long string, it makes a whirring noise like the noise a flying whale might make with its wings. Suddenly I understand why it scares the wolves so. Deep down in their souls, the wolves remember a time when flying whales used to eat their kind.

Jukku holds the wolf-scare high, but he doesn't swing it round and round to make the sound because there is not enough room in the tent. Instead he makes a noise with his mouth and we all laugh, because Jukku's mouth sounds nothing like a wolf-scare.

The tent door slaps open and Nagazruk shoves his head inside. The look on his face stifles our laughter.

They are out there, he whispers. *The wolves. They are circling.*

His words make the tiny hairs on my arms stand on end. We all file out of the tent, one by one, and it is clear at once that the deer are nervous. They are no longer feeding peacefully in the valley below us. Instead, they are inching their way closer and closer to the tent, until it seems as though they will soon crush us. They are so close we can hear the sound of their breathing, labored and frightened in the dark.

At first I see nothing of the wolves. But as my eyes grow accustomed to the night, the eyes of the wolves begin to pop out of the darkness at the far edge of the herd, like little yellow flames. I turn around slowly, following the string of yellow eyes, one by one, and I see that it's true: the wolves have formed a ring around us. We are surrounded.

There's an inner ring and an outer ring, Nagazruk says in a low voice.

I squint my eyes hard into the darkness but I cannot see the outer ring. I see only the flash, here and there, of more eyes and wish, suddenly, that I were back home in Auntie Ubliuk's house, sewing. I wish this with all my heart.

Jukku pulls his wolf-scare from his pocket and Nagazruk does the same, as does Amaġuq. There are only three of them—three boys swinging wolf-scares over the tops of their heads as they run out toward the ring of wolves, each running in a different direction. The whirring sound the wolf-scares make is high-pitched and menacing. It sounds like a thick swarm of angry insects, surging in the air around us.

One by one the eyes of the wolves blink—then disappear—and I stand there in the twinkling dark, breathing deeply once again.

In the morning, when we wake up, the deer are again

down in the valley below, nuzzling the tundra grass peacefully, as though nothing has happened.

Deer, I think, have very short memories and do not pay attention, for long, to things of danger. That is why they must have herders, I suppose.

I think suddenly of my sister, crossing to the other side of the ocean in the Siberian's boat. Have they been overtaken by a storm? Are the dark clouds swooping down on them like cruel birds? Is their little boat being tossed about among big black swells like a shred of grass? I wish my mind were able to escape worry the way a reindeer's can. Life is short, their big dark eyes seem to say; why fear that which is yet to come?

I am suddenly torn by a desire both to protect the deer and to become one with them. We are the animals we eat, Aaka says, and right now, deep down inside, I feel both the peace and the terror of the deer.

BACK HOME in the village, we hang the newly harvested reindeer skins out to dry in the cold wind. The fur is thick, as it always is in the fall. They will make fine, warm mattresses, these skins, and there's enough for all of us to have new ones, too. Mama is very merry, making bread to celebrate and fixing a fine meal of my favorite soup, made from the tongue and head of the reindeer. My cousins have gone back to camp, but I am to stay here and help the women. And I am not sad for this. We are so rich with new skins and meat that it is good to sit indoors as the snow flies. The sun is above the horizon for only a few moments these days before it sinks again into darkness, and I would just as soon sit cozy and content in Auntie Ubliuk's house, playing with chubby little Manu, than huddled in a flapping tent surrounded by wolves.

Auntie's winter house is warm and snug, blanketed with sod. The sod covers the house so that when you look from a distance it seems like no more than a hill on the tundra. Inside, everything is hushed and secure, covered by snow and tundra and well protected from wolves and dark spirits and the fierce winds of winter, already blowing.

I have nearly ceased missing the sound of the herd when one afternoon I see my cousin Nagazruk heading toward us, running hard. He is returning from herding much earlier than we had expected.

Nagazruk is, of course, always running hard, running like the wind with his deer, running for the fun of it, as I do. But this time there is no fun at all in his run. I can see this, even from a distance. I see, in the way he holds his head down, that he has something important to attend to and is determined to arrive quickly, noticing nothing along the way. As though he is bound to bring us the news he holds and bring it fast.

It is not good news.

Sickness is spreading up and down the coast like a swarm of mosquitoes, he says. It is devouring whole villages in a dark shadow of death. Several of the smaller villages no longer even exist, he tells us, still breathless from running. The smallest villages stand silent, their houses stopped shut with the bodies of the dead. This is what a hunter passing through has told him.

Nagazruk talks fast, his eyes bright with fear. His words make my heart beat hard. We must be very careful not to bring sickness to our village. We must follow the old ways, staying away from the houses of the dead.

We must listen to the shaman, Uncle Saġġan says.

I feel cold clear through, as though our village is surrounded by a thick ring of wolves in the cold winter darkness. I wish we could hang polar bear bones on all the four corners of my mother's village, to scare off the spirits of sickness. I wish I could drape all the homes with blue beads and pull a sealskin over us and fool death with a loud voice. I wish I could run out from the center of the village, swinging a wolf-scare as wide as a mountain, run as far north as the village of my father's people.

I try to think of Uyaġak, the rock, and of the strong words he used to marry my sister, words that he said were stronger than even the shaman's, but the sounds stick in my throat like feathers of fear.

Fly past us, sickness; do not land on our village. Do not touch us.

Nippivik—in the-time-when-the-sun-sets

Mail

Mail is arriving from Kawarek, a sledload thick with mail. We watch it appear on the horizon like a ghost in the dusky afternoon light. Perhaps it is sugar or flour or tea. Or maybe it is clothes such as the boot-sole people wear, sent by the teachers who sometimes come to teach us their ways. And maybe, just maybe, there is news from our island and beyond—a letter from the Russian side, with word of my sister. We run out to meet the mailman, racing one another to be first, laughing for the joy of it.

The mailman is driving his dog team straight toward the center of town. He has two sisters in this village and they are excited to see him, too, running out with the rest of us, running just like us kids even though they are both nearly old enough to be *aakas* themselves. We all want the mailman to come to our own houses, of course, want him to shake the snow from his parka by our own doors and give us treats from the packages on his sled, laughing loudly at his own silly jokes. But as we get closer we see that there is no smile on the mailman's face. Something is wrong, very wrong. My father is running now, too, trying to outrun us all, hollering out warnings.

Wait! Stop! Stay away! Stay away!

But no one listens. Even I do not listen, running ahead of all the others, refusing to hear Papa, thinking only of my sister and hoping for news of her, pretending I can't hear the note of alarm in my father's voice; pretending it doesn't scare me at all to hear him holler as if we are about to be swallowed up by a wall of ice. And because I'm the fastest, I'm first to arrive at the sled, first to see the truth: there is no mail on the mailman's sled, no mail at all.

The mailman's sled is not loaded with fine goods and new wonders; it carries, instead, a young boy, the mailman's son, bundled up in skins and lying prone. As I get closer, I see that he shakes with cold even though he is well covered with skins. He is sick, I realize with a sudden icy feeling. The smoke of his breath in the frozen air is thin and puny and his eyes are glazed.

The sickness has come to our village after all, come wrapped up in skins on the mailman's sled: a skinny boy my own age with no look of recognition in his eyes, gazing out at us as though he doesn't quite believe we are real, as though he has already entered the world of the dead.

THE BOY'S NAME was Tuqua and he died the next morning. We did not have to be told he had died; we could hear it in the wailing of the two women who were his aunties. The men have blocked both the door and the nose of the house where he died. No one will enter there again.

But they cannot block out the sickness. The sickness has settled over my mother's village like greasy smoke.

Siqiñģiļaq—in the-time-when-there-is-no-sun

The Fourth Disaster

Baby Manu is not laughing anymore. Her mama is sick and Manu just sits there on the floor whimpering, while her mama shakes with sickness on the sleeping loft above her. I cannot bear the sound of it, but when I pick her up she just clings to me with frightened eyes, still whimpering.

I am one of the few who has not taken sick and I keep myself too busy to think by going from house to house to help the sick ones, cleaning their beds and spooning thin soup into the mouths of those too weak to feed themselves. It is a sad job, but my cousin Nagazruk's job is even sadder—he and Tupaaq are hauling off the bodies of those who have died. We can no longer afford to seal the houses of the dead: we, the living, would have no place left to go.

The boys have no time left to tend to the herd, these days. We are all too busy tending to the village. Right now I wish more than anything that I could run out to the camp, run and run with the deer, outrunning the wolves and the mailman and all the news I do not want to hear, all the bad news. But of course I can't outrun it. This sickness is too big to run from. This sickness has settled over top of us like a heavy rotting skin, as wide as the sky, suffocating every village it encounters. Even ours.

Like me, Tupaaq remains untouched by sickness. He is hauling away the dead by the sledload, still as strong as ever. But the smile that used to close his eyes with happiness is gone, replaced by a wide-eyed gaze that sees nothing. I watch him driving back and forth with his loads of death, his eyes blank as snow, looking as if the whole world has disappeared into a fog. Which is exactly how it feels to me, too. The very air itself feels thick with death, so thick that I sometimes find myself gasping and gasping for fresh air like a fish on the beach.

Where do they take them, these sledloads of the dead? I do not want to even think of it.

Mama and Papa are coughing now, too, and I can't bear to stay in Auntie's house for long, watching the way Papa's strong hands have grown too weak to hold a cup of broth. Watching Mama's eyes, so glassy with fever that she fails, at times, to see me. Fails even to notice when I talk.

I have escaped to Baby Manu's house, but it is just the same here. I hold the baby while I try to feed her mama, but Manu's mama won't swallow the soup I give her, so the warm broth just dribbles down her chin like tears. Manu clings to me with skinny arms, her tiny body taut with fear. When it comes time to leave, I resolve to take her with me, but as soon as I begin to descend into the entry, she cries out in terror, reaching up for her mama with a pathetic little sound that hardly even sounds like crying, so I settle her into the loft next to her mama and tuck the skins around them both. Manu sticks her thumb into her mouth and hunkers down, eyes half closed, making pathetic little sucking sounds. There is barely enough oil left to keep the lamp burning through the night and when I check in the storage room I see there is not a single chunk of blubber left. I will have to bring some from Auntie's house when I return. I trim the lamp's wick carefully, feeling Manu's little eyes watching, but when I lean down to smile at her, she gazes up at me blankly, as though she has forgotten who I am. I climb down out of the room and crawl through the entry, tears gathering in the back of my throat. They sting my eyes and freeze to my cheeks like a mask of sadness as I walk across the village to Auntie's house.

The whole village is silent. The kind of silence that makes me want to run toward the mountains howling, mournful as a wolf.

I WAKE SLOWLY the next morning, wishing I could remain lost forever in the forgetfulness of sleep, but before the sleep has even left me, I'm aware of the tightness in my chest, the tightness that was with me when I fell asleep, the tightness that will remain always, I fear. Before I open my eyes I remember, suddenly, the lamp in Manu's house and resolve to bring blubber there immediately, before the light goes out and the house grows cold. But as soon as I open my eyes, another awareness begins to dawn on me. Our house is far too quiet—something is missing.

Papa's snoring!

Papa's snoring is gone—Papa, who last night was far too sick to go hunting, too sick to roll over without help. Too sick to even eat. I sit up quickly and look toward his sleeping loft, wondering where he has gone.

But Papa is still there. His big form fills the loft as solid as ever, but his body is still, as still as stone. The familiar sounds he makes when he turns and moves are gone.

My papa, too, is gone.

Papa!

All I can think of is his laugh, his big drumlike laugh, pounding in my dreams. Back in the time when I used to have dreams, sleeping on the skins at Mama's feet, comforted, even in my sleep, by the sound of Papa's laughter. But now it's gone.

My papa and his laughter are gone.

I don't know how long I sit there on the floor, watching. Mama lies on her skins, barely moving, completely unaware of the fact that Papa has left us. Auntie sits in the corner, sobbing quietly, and when the boys come to take Papa's body away I want to pound them with my fists, but of course I do not. Tupaaq stands there watching me with a look so sad and defeated I cannot even bear to meet his eyes. Instead, I turn my face to the wall where Mama lies. And when Tupaaq moves toward me as if to comfort me, I move even further away. I don't know why I do this. Part of me wants, more than anything, to feel Tupaaq's big protecting arms around me, wiping my fear away. But another part of me wants to turn from everyone and everything and nurture my own pain, all alone, like a wolf.

After they leave with Papa's body, it feels as if the whole world has left and suddenly I want, more than anything, to shake Mama awake as she lies there, distant as a piece of driftwood, drifting calmly away on a tide of death, totally oblivious of my sobs. I want to shake her away from this foggy place we are lost in, shake her back into the world of the living. Shake and shake and shake. Instead I reach for a bowl of cold broth and try to feed her. But she turns her head to the wall as though even the thought of food sickens her, turns her head weakly as though even the weight of her own head has suddenly become unbearable. Outside, I hear the sound of the boys leaving with Papa's body—the yipping of the dogs and the scraping of the sled's runners and the sharp-edged pitch of Auntie's voice crying out across the thin frozen air. I think Mama hears them, too—for just a moment—as she stares toward the wall. Stares toward the place where Papa has gone, her eyes unblinking.

The realization hits me slowly—Mama has turned her head away forever. Mama will never ever turn her head back toward me, never ever look again on the living. Mama has followed Papa.

Mama!

I push my way outside the house, pushing against the heavy weight of death that presses down upon me.

Mama!

My eyes feel blind in the freezing darkness of early morning, as though I have been buried alive beneath a heavy piece of ice with my eyes wide open. The ice is so thick and so heavy I will never be able to move it, never again breathe deeply, never see, again, the world of the living through living eyes. The ice has frozen my heart solid and I feel numb, completely numb.

Suddenly I remember Manu, lying alone with her dying mama in a cold dark house, and the thought moves me to action. I climb back down into the entrance to our house as if in a daze, moving into the storage room, hardly even aware of what I am doing. I see the frozen blubber on a shelf in the cold room, see the big *ulu*, the one Auntie always uses to slice blubber, and I watch my hand cutting off a piece for Manu's lamp, watching as if I am watching someone else's actions. My legs climb up out of the house and my feet walk across the village, straight to Manu's house. I walk slow and steady, but part of me is not really here. Part of me watches from a distance, as if it is another girl doing all these things, another girl, blank as snow, a girl whose heart is too frozen to feel anything. I watch her trudge the distance, my own heart beating with a sharp, icy pain, slowly, very slowly.

With every step I take, I have to remind myself to keep breathing, and with every breath I take, I wish I didn't have to.

Aaka said there were three disasters. I remember this now, watching from this lonely distance. There was the Great Cold, which only four families survived, and the Great Flood, which only three survived, and the Great Starvation, which scoured the land nearly clean of people. And now this—sickness. Sickness crushing us like heavy ice, the fourth disaster, Death.

The Great Death.

IT IS TOO LATE for blubber—the lamp at Manu's house has gone out and the room is cold. When my eyes adjust to the dim light that falls from the skylight, I see Manu lying still, next to her lifeless mother, her tiny thumb stuck in her mouth like a stone, her eyes as blank as Mama's.

The silence of death has become as familiar as family. I recognize it instantly. I want to run but my legs are frozen, so

I just stand there, the image of that room burning itself onto the backs of my eyelids. It's an image that will remain there forever: Baby Manu, gone around the bend from life to death, lying there by her mama, her little thumb frozen into her mouth forever. I take the string of beads from my neck, the two beads Aaluk has given me, and remove one, tucking it into Baby Manu's clenched little fist. My beads—I am giving this one to Manu. The other I will always keep to remember Aaluk by.

I want that one big bead to fool death. I want, more than anything I will ever again want, to fool death! But when I walk out of Manu's house, the cold feeling in the base of my chest tells me that it is foolish to ever again want anything at all.

Siqiññaatchiaq—in the-time-of-the-bright-new-sun

The Ones We Lost

Mama.
Papa.
Aaka.
Manu.
Ubliuk.
Even Nagazruk.
Nearly all the babies,
and all the old ones, with the old knowledge
we never yet
learned.
Nuna and her sweet, sweet baby,
a boy. Even Ayałhuq,
so strong she could shoot an arrow farther than Tupaaq. Even her
we lost.
Sickness, taking everyone around the last bend,
even our own future,
gone.

Now there is nothing left.
No big families, only broken pieces
of families, a woman
who used to be a mother, a child
who used to have parents, a brother
no longer called Brother,
all of us
drifting
somewhere in between,
a foggy sea without land.
I am no one's daughter,
no one's granddaughter,
no one's.

More than anything else, I want my sister, Aaluk, want to know
that this terrible thing has not taken her, too, has not followed her
to the far side of the dim horizon.
     Aaluk!

The meat supplies are dwindling fast—nearly gone—but we haven't the heart to tend to the herd, haven't the heart to even eat. I myself am not at all hungry and cannot even remember what it feels like to desire food. Everything left here on this earth tastes like sand, cold sand on a lost island in a foggy sea.

One of the boot-sole leaders has come to us—too late to be of any help. He calls for a meeting at the schoolhouse, to do what, I cannot imagine. There is nothing left to do, nothing left for those of us who remain living save to trudge through the deep snows of life, alone. I go down to the schoolhouse where I never went to school, dressed in my new parka, remembering, as though recalling one of the old stories, how happy I once felt wearing it. It is still very pretty, and perhaps I even look as pretty as Auntie told me I did, but being pretty matters even less to me now than it did before.

Of what use is beauty in a world so disfigured by death?

It is a warm parka, too, with soft downy skins on the inside, but today I feel cold wearing it.

Cold. Cold. Cold.

Perhaps I will never again know warmth. This is what I really believe, standing here in the chilly schoolhouse with all the others, shivering. I'm listening to the boot-sole leader talking, wishing I had been more diligent in learning the boot-sole language, the one they call Ing-lish. Where is Tupaaq? Tupaaq, who always understands everybody. Suddenly I miss Tupaaq as though he has died, which, thankfully, he has not.

But where is he?

We are divided into two groups, the men and boys on one side, girls and women on the other. The boot-sole leader stands between us, waving papers. Speaking so loud and so fast he grows red in the face from the effort.

He wants to marry us, the girl standing next to me whispers. She is one of the ones who truly understands this new language. She understands because she had lived with one of the teachers, caring for the teacher's children. The rest of us sidle over next to her to learn what is being said.

Marry who? someone whispers.

Us. The men and the women. All of us.

I want to mention that not all of us are really women yet, but think better of it when I realize that the girl speaking is younger than me and has tears glittering in her eyes.

He wants us to make new families, she whispers in a quivering voice. *He wants us to pick spouses . . . all of us . . . right now.*

Just like that he wants us to pick spouses for ourselves from the herd of men and boys who stand silently watching us from across the room. It sounds absurd, like a silly game we might play, laughing merrily for the fun of it. Only it isn't a game and it isn't at all funny.

And besides, we have forgotten how to laugh.

Some couples have begun to form, just as they were told to do. These are the ones who appear to have already had spouses in mind. The rest of us just stand together, dumb as deer, while this strange man begins to pair us off, man to woman.

The youngest girls have begun to cry. You would hardly recognize it as crying, though, because they don't make a sound. They are too scared, all of them, to even move, their cheeks growing shiny with silent tears. Old man Aŋaayyuk—married to his wife longer than anyone could remember—is paired off with little Uiñiq, who never even got to bury her parents and all five of her brothers. Uiñiq, young enough to be Aŋaayyuk's granddaughter.

As the leader moves down the line of men, pairing other girls off with other men, I want to turn around and run from the building. Run out across the tundra, running faster than every last one of the men, especially that ruddy-faced boot-sole leader, so thick and blustering. But, in fact, I remain motionless, unable to move, stuck to this one spot as though my feet are frozen to the floor. By the time my turn comes, I have nearly quit breathing altogether. The leader looks at me and then looks across the room at Maksik, who stands there leering at me in a slow, greasy sort of way. Maksik, who for good reason has never had a wife of his own. The air in the room feels suddenly thin and stale and a wave of nausea washes over me.

You! the leader says, pointing at me. Pointing in a way so rude it would make the old women click their tongues and shake their heads in warning.

Were there any old women left to warn us.

He says the next couple will adopt three of the parentless children, the girl next to me whispers.

Suddenly, from behind me, comes a voice I recognize.

I'll take that one!

Tupaaq! He is speaking in the boot-sole language, and even though I am not sure of the individual words, I understand what he is saying. I can feel it, the meaning of his words, feel it deep inside.

I will marry this one, he adds in our own language, hooking his big arm around me. *This one is mine.*

I look up at Tupaaq, towering over me, and before I can think about what I am about to do, I say these words, firm and final: *I am not Aaluk.*

I say it just as she would have said it, too: with pride and certainty.

I am not the one you want. I am Nutaaq.

Then, looking across the room at Maksik, I am suddenly stricken with the knowledge of my own foolishness. I tighten my jaw, waiting for the boot-sole leader to seal my fate. But before anyone can say a thing, there is laughter, laughter of a kind we no longer believed possible, certainly not in a place such as this.

Tupaaq's laughter, nearly as deep as Papa's, echoes out across the cold, cramped room.

No, my little lemming, you are not Aaluk, he says, standing there smiling his shut-eye smile. *You are not at all Aaluk.*

And suddenly I, too, am smiling, smiling all the way down to my toes.

Will you let me take you home? Tupaaq asks.

Home.

I thought I would never again feel within me the meaning of that word. And I know, without asking, that for Tupaaq, home is the place where his own people live, far to the north. Tupaaq's home is not our little island, now so empty of people. And somehow this, too, feels right. Completely right.

Yes, I say. *Yes, I will.*

Home to the-place-where-they-hunt-snowy-owls, Tupaaq whispers.

Home to the village of my father's people.

I look up at Tupaaq, the way a grown woman would look at her man, realizing suddenly that I *am* a grown woman— one of the oldest ones left. My hand goes instinctively to my chin. Who will mark me now, with a woman's tattoo? There is no one left.

I will wear, instead, the mark of a survivor. We all will.

Grandma Aaluk Ends the Story

*T*hey were married right there in that room, my mother, Nutaaq, wearing the parka she and her aunt had made, the one that became a wedding parka, after all. A very fine parka, indeed. And they adopted three of the children—three of the little boys who had lost their parents. These are my older brothers Joseph, Noah, and Isaac.

We have this one picture of the two of them together, Nutaaq and Tupaaq, as they might have looked on the day they were married, both in reindeer-skin parkas with fancy trim, smiling the bittersweet smile of survivors. This photo, of course, was taken much later, right before I was born—long after they had moved north.

We don't have any other photos of this time. We have only the story as my mother, Nutaaq, has told it; this story as I, Nutaaq's daughter—your aaka Aaluk—have remembered it.

Book II
Blessing's Story
1989

August in Anchorage, Alaska

My mom always braid my hair before she go Bingo sometimes and she always say knock-knock jokes to make me laugh. And stories, too, sometimes, stories about lemmings and witches and the northern lights.

Back home in Anchorage.

My mom always make the kind of braid that go all the way round my head like a crown, all right. I like that kind best, all right.

When I wear that kind to Sunday school, everybody wants their hairs that way, too, but their moms don't know how, only mine.

But when my mom go Bingo, Stephan always drink beer sometimes and beer makes Stephan mad. When Stephan go beer-mad he sings loud about ninety-nine bottles of beer on the wall. And use the F word. A lot.

When Mom comes home from Bingo, Stephan says F Bingo and when Isaac and me comes home from Sunday school, he says F Jesus Christ. And when Mom drinks beer she says bad things, too. She says Stephan could go hell and good riddance.

Pastor Sellers says people who go hell burn forever with other people who scream and cry all night long in the fire.

Stephan says he gonna go hell, all right, and he gonna take us with him. He even try take my mom, pulling her arm wrong way till she cry, but she don't go because I jump on Stephan's back to make him stop. Even though Mom says not to.

Stephan shoves me to the floor, shoves me right into the empty beer cans. His elbow hits my eye hard and my shoulder knocks the picture off the wall, the real old one of my great-grandma Nutaaq and my great-grandpa Tupaaq; the ones me and Isaac got named after.

Run! Mom screams. *Run away!*

But I can't move.

The people who live above us are pounding on the floor loud, but nobody cares because Mom's too busy screaming and Stephan's cussing and Isaac is crying real hard. Isaac's afraid to go hell. But he's even more afraid of Stephan.

All the sounds bang at my ears and my eye is burning bad and the glass from that picture is all over the floor in sharp pieces. I tell Isaac not to move and he holds my hand tight. Isaac don't want to go hell with Stephan.

But none of us gonna go hell. Stephan gonna go jail and Mom gonna go hospital and me and Isaac gonna go with this lady who says she takes care of kids like us, this lady with hair the color of cornflakes.

Mom is holding on to her arm and crying and cussing at

that lady. That lady who don't even ask if we want to go. She just takes us.

ME AND ISAAC do not want to be kids-like-us.

The place where kids-like-us go got lots of beds and no windows and we can't leave. There's no moms there, either, only kids. They give us spaghetti and both me and Isaac likes spaghetti, all right, but we like it better hot.

When it's time to go bed, they don't let me and Isaac go together. Isaac cries and cries. He have to go with the boys and he don't want to. I can still feel him crying when I go to the girls' room. I want to cry, too, all right, but I can't. My tears got turned inside out, somehow, and now they can't come out no more.

In the morning they take us to a room with a desk full of papers. A tall man points to the chairs and tells us to sit there. Me and Isaac sits on one chair together. We don't look at the man. We look at the pictures on his wall. One is a picture of words with fancy writing and another is a picture of a mom with two girls. The girls got yellow hair and pink sweatshirts and it looks like they been laughing. The man coughs and says something to the papers on his desk.

Then he looks up, looks right at me with his eyes, which are gray-colored, and his mouth, which does not smile.

You have a grandmother who lives up North, he says. I nod because I already know we got a grandma up North. *Grandma* is how white people say *aaka*.

Isaac don't say nothing. He just sits there looking at his fingers like maybe he don't hear or don't know how to talk, but he does.

We're gonna go live with our grandma, that man tells us. Which is only a *temporary solution to our situation*. I nod again, even though I am not sure what that means. Isaac is trying hard not to cry, I could tell. Isaac's thinking the same as me: What about our mom? What happens to the moms of kids-like-us?

Isaac and me is afraid to go up North alone because we don't even know our *aaka*. Especially not Isaac, who was born in Anchorage and never even seen her before.

Not like me. I was born in the village, even if I don't remember. That's where I got my Eskimo name, Nutaaq. That's the name of my mom's grandma, the one who raised her. The one my mom calls Mom. The one that died. How come my mom wasn't raised by her own mom, my *aaka*? That's what I want to know.

Because, Mom says when I ask. And that's all she ever says, too: *because*.

I'm thinking about that word *because*, sitting here in this office that smells like paper and looking at this man who don't smile. *Because* is not a word that makes you feel good about leaving your real mom in Anchorage and getting on a plane to go up North to live with your *aaka* you don't even remember. An *aaka* your mom never calls Mom even though she really is her mom. *Because* is not a word you could hang on to at a time like this.

We are going to have to fly in a plane, too, because flying is the only way to get to Aaka's village. There are no roads and no other way in or out except by plane.

Plane tickets cost too much, Mom used to say when we asked why we can't go visit.

And that's all she ever said, too.

Aaka's Village

When we fly away from Anchorage, it's summer. When we land at Aaka's village, it feels like fall. That fast. Summer blows off the Anchorage runway in a puff of black smoke and fall flies into our noses when we land. The plane roars down the runway, rattling and clanging like a bunch of big keys, bumping back and forth.

Whoa, big boy, the stewardess says, *whoa.* Like she could talk to the plane. But the plane don't hardly listen because outside the wind talks louder than the plane. Outside, the wind talks against the side of the plane like a big old man with a rusty throat. Outside the wind is trying to make the plane keep flying off to someplace else. But there is no place else. We already flew over all the frozen white mountains and all the flat wide tundra and all the rivers, curvy as snakes. Now we are at the edge of the ocean, where all you could see is ice and more ice.

There is no place else left to go. This is the end.

When the plane finally stops for good, we have to climb down the plane stairs and walk right into that wind, which blows so hard it wraps my hairs around my face and knocks Isaac's hat right off his head. I try run catch it, but before I can, a big man reaches out and grabs it. Grabs Isaac's hat right off the wind. Then he looks down and smiles at us and messes Isaac's hairs. I take Isaac's hand and pull him away. I don't like strangers messing my little brother's hairs.

Wind got a mind of her own, the man says, winking at the wind. Like the wind is his girlfriend. This man who's big enough to be the wind's honey, walking right next to us, holding Isaac's hat while the wind pushes us into the airport with big cold hands.

Inside is a bunch of people all hunched up together and it's cold. Isaac stops right there at the door and the people coming in almost step on him. I pull at his arm.

Don't stop, I say, even though I want to stop, too. Stop, then run. Run away, just like Mom said. Run right back to the playground where Mom used to tell me knock-knock jokes and I used to be happy.

Before Stephan.

Blessing! a voice says. *Isaac!* It's a scratchy old voice that reaches right straight through all the people and all the noise and pokes our shoulders with sharp fingers.

Aaka.

She's wearing a parka that got big purple and yellow flowers all over it with dark brown fur at the top and bottom, and her hair is white and puffy like cotton. Her eyes look right past us, like she don't even see us, pushing through the crowd of people, calling our names.

Isaac pulls behind me, trying to hide.

That's Aaka, I whisper. Isaac don't remember Aaka. Me neither.

Nutaaq? Tupaaq?

She's almost whispering now. Like how the wind would sound if the wind could whisper. But I like the way she says our names, our Eskimo names, me and Isaac's: Nutaaq and Tupaaq. In Anchorage they never say our names.

That big man steps up next to us and I pull Isaac off the way quick.

These Rose's kids? he asks Aaka. Aaka says something in Eskimo, which I don't understand, and that man puts his big fat hand on the top of my head.

I grab Isaac's hand so hard Isaac goes, *Ow!*

I don't like big men who put their hands on the tops of kids' heads.

You two gotta call me Uncle, the man tells us.

Then he reaches into his pocket and pulls out a pack of gum. He don't say anything, just peels back the paper and holds it out to us. I shake my head no, but Isaac grabs it quick without hardly looking and stuffs it into his mouth. That gum is almost too big for his mouth. I kick Isaac with my foot, real soft, where no one could see.

U-cle, Isaac says, his mouth full of gum.

Uncle laughs a big pounding laugh.

Come on, kids, Aaka says. *Your uncle gonna give us a ride home.*

UNCLE'S TRUCK clangs like a garbage truck, bouncing up and down on the dusty roads of Aaka's village. Me and Isaac and

Aaka bounce, too, up and down on the hard seat. We drive right next to the ocean, which has giant waves smashing into the beach and white ice, way out far, and one giant piece of blue-green ice, bobbing in the waves by the beach. That one ice is bigger than Uncle's truck and looks like it got a green-blue light deep down inside.

Here you go, Auntie Aaluk, Uncle says, stopping his truck in front of a house which got red paint on it in some places but is mostly just wood-color. Like all the paint got blowed off by the wind.

Aaka's house is right by the beach, so close you could feel the waves pounding, but it doesn't sit on the ground like the houses in Anchorage—it sits up on top of fat poles so you could see right underneath it. All the other houses around are just like that, too.

How come these houses got legs? Isaac says.

Those are pilings, Uncle says.

There's also black meat hanging from a piece of wood by the door and Isaac is looking at it with big eyes. That meat is ribs, like the ribs of a long skinny kid, which makes me think about that story where the kids get lost in the woods and go to a witch's house and the witch tries to eat them. I'm glad there's no woods here.

Isaac stands there staring at those ribs, without moving.

What's that? he says.

I poke him to be quiet, even though I want to know, too.

Tuttu. Uncle says. *Caribou.*

Paniqtaq, Aaka says. *Dry caribou. You gonna like it.*

Isaac wrinkles his nose, but Aaka doesn't see because Aaka is busy getting out of the truck with Uncle helping her.

Uncle looks at me. *And which one are you?* he says.

She's Blessing, Isaac offers.

Nutaaq, Aaka says.

Nutaaq, Uncle says, like he's waiting for me to say it, too.
But I don't.

Pictures and Names

The first thing I notice about Aaka's house is all the pictures. There's pictures on the walls, on the tables, on the refrigerator, pictures everywhere. How many? Maybe a hundred. Maybe two hundred. Some got gold or brown frames and some got frames that say things like *Grandma's Baby* or *Best Friends*. Some don't got any frames at all.

Aaka's pictures cram every space, everywhere, and the first thing I do is just stand there staring. Isaac, too. Isaac never seen so many pictures before and the first thing he does is say, *Whoa, pictures!* Then he starts counting.

One, two, three, four, five, six, seven, eight . . .

Isaac could count real good for a little kid, all right.

That's our family. Aaka says, smiling. But she's smiling at her pictures, not at us.

The way Aaka is smiling at those pictures is like she's looking at real people, people who are standing right here in this room, breathing our same air and remembering about the fun things they all did yesterday or last week.

But when I look, all I see is pictures. Pictures of strangers I never even met. There's brown-colored pictures of people in brown fur parkas and white-colored ones of men with dark faces standing in the snow wearing white parkas. And lots of pictures of groups of people smiling at each other and lots of school pictures of kids all different ages, some without their front teeth.

Then I see one picture of people I know. It's a picture of my mom holding a baby, and that baby is me. The frame says *Babies Are a Blessing from God.*

. . . *seventeen, eighteen, nineteen, twenty*, Isaac says.

Maybe I got my name Blessing from that picture. Maybe my mom saw that frame and thought Blessing was a good name for a baby. I really like the way Mom is smiling in that picture. Like everything in the world is happy. I can't stop staring at the way my mom's smiling. Smiling in some happy place I can't remember.

. . . *fifty-one, fifty-two, fifty-three*, Isaac says.

Aaka reaches out and runs her finger along the edge of the frame I'm looking at, right where it says *Babies Are a Blessing from God* in bumpy letters.

Your mom sure was happy that time, Aaka says. *She always happy back then.*

The way Aaka says *back then* makes it sound like another country.

Blessing's the name I gave you, Aaka says.

This surprises me, but I don't say it.

Your mom tell you how come she name you Nutaaq?

I raise my eyebrows to say yes. I know why Mom named me Nutaaq. She named me Nutaaq because that's her grandma's name—her grandma-mom, not her real mom. Not Aaka. I look at Aaka. And Aaka looks right back at me, but her eyes aren't looking at me. Her eyes look someplace else, someplace I can't see.

She named me Nutaaq because Nutaaq was her mom, I say, even though I know it isn't true. Nutaaq wasn't really her mom. Nutaaq was her *aaka*, my great-grandma.

Aaka breathes a short quick breath like she stepped on something sharp.

My mom, Nutaaq, she died right after you were born, Aaka says.

For some reason, I think about that old picture of my great-grandparents, the one my mom had. And then, like a song you can't quit hearing, I remember all the broken glass on the floor when Stephan made me knock that picture off the wall that time.

. . . ninety-eight, ninety-nine.

I give Isaac a hard look to try make him shut up.

Stop it, Isaac. Quit counting.

Aaka frowns. *He could count if he wants to.*

Isaac grins. *Who did I get named after?* he asks.

Tupaaq, Aaka says. *That's my dad's name.* Aaka looks up and smiles, like she could see her dad standing right there in front of her.

That makes you my little dad, Eskimo way, she says.

Isaac giggles. *I'm hungry,* he says, trying to make his voice sound deep like a dad's. He follows Aaka into the kitchen and I follow him. You could still hear the wind outside, banging against the side of the house like a big old drunk, trying to find the door.

Aaka puts a box of Sailor Boy crackers and a can of jam on the table. Sailor Boy makes me think of Mom because back home in Anchorage we always have Sailor Boy. Sailor Boy is *all* we have sometimes. Sailor Boy crackers and peanut butter, the kind we buy with food stamps.

How come the wind blow so hard? Isaac asks.

Aaka is fixing tea. We watch her stir spoons of sugar into her cup.

Fall storms they like that, Aaka says.

When we go bed the fall storm is blowing so loud it makes the windows of Aaka's house rattle like a giant making popcorn somewhere close. Me and Isaac sleep in one bed, which Aaka says is ours. The wind pushes Aaka's house back and forth on its pilings so hard I keep thinking we gonna fall off. Isaac puts his head under the blanket and lies real still. He's scared.

It's okay, I tell Isaac. *It's just like being on a boat. Right?*

Isaac nods even though he's never been on a boat before.

Feel how the waves are lifting us up and down?

Isaac nods again. Then he puts his head up on my pillow and shuts his eyes, satisfied. *Could we go Disneyland on the boat?* he whispers.

We could go anywhere on a boat, I tell him. *We could go to a brand-new world where the houses are made of cookies and the clouds are Cool Whip,* I tell him.

Me and Mom used to pretend sometimes that we were on clouds made out of Cool Whip. Clouds that could move fast, way up high where only me and Mom could go.

What color is your cloud? Mom always used to whisper sometimes.

Butterscotch, I'd say. Butterscotch is my favorite color for a cloud.

But the clouds above Aaka's village are not butterscotch-colored. Aaka's clouds are gray as *cigaaq* smoke, and the wind out there is ripping them to pieces. I could hear it. This makes me think of Mom and Stephan again. When I close my eyes, I could even hear Mom's voice in the wind: *Run! Run away!*

All of a sudden, Aaka's house jerks like somebody big is bumping it with their butt. I jump, but Isaac don't even notice because Isaac's asleep. That's how little kids are. You can get them to quit thinking about scary things real easy. Then they go to sleep without hardly trying. Not me. I'm wide awake, lying on my back in the windy dark, holding on tight to the bed. Thinking hard.

Aaka name me Blessing, but Mom don't ever call me that now because I'm not. *Pakak* fits me better. That's what Mom says. A *pakak* is someone who gets into things, like puppies do. Or little kids. When you *pakak*, people always say: *Araa! Don't pakak!*

But Sister is what Mom calls me most: *Sit still, Sister,* or *Make Baby cereal, Sister.* Baby is what my mom calls Isaac even though he isn't. Not anymore. No one but Aaka calls me Nutaaq. And Uncle.

Isaac rolls off the pillow and curls up against my side. Pretty soon I stop thinking so hard and quit noticing the wind so much. After a while I let the wind rock me back and forth, real gentle, and I close my eyes. It sounds like the wind is calling out my name now, too. My Eskimo name: *Nuuu-taq, Nuuuuuu-taq.*

Pakak

All night long the wind blows and blows and the house sways back and forth in my dreams like a big black ship. One time I wake up and it feels like there's something crawling along the dark floor, trying to get me. Even Isaac stirs in his sleep and opens his eyes quick, like he could feel something, too. For a few dark seconds, he looks at me wide-eyed, but then he curls down underneath the covers and puts his arm around my waist and we let the wind rock us back to sleep again.

I dream that the wind is a big broom, sweeping things clean.

IN THE MORNING, I wake up first. Isaac is still sleeping, curled up like a puppy, and Aaka is snoring real soft, which I could hear now because the wind's gone and the sun is shining. The house is so quiet I'm afraid to even breathe too hard. I go into the living room, trying not to make any noise. It's spooky, sitting all alone with Aaka's pictures staring at me like maybe they think I shouldn't be here. Like they know, somehow, I don't belong.

Outside the window, seagulls are flying back and forth across the sky with voices that sound like rusty doors opening and closing. I sit on Aaka's couch, watching them fly, little white bits of light against the blue sky.

I look at the refrigerator, humming in the kitchen, and my stomach growls, but all those faces taped on the refrigerator door look right back at me and they all say the same thing: *Don't pakak.*

I look down. There's a big can of cookies on the living room table. That can's so big you could probably take a bunch of cookies out without anyone even noticing. I look back at Aaka's room, which is dark, and I take the lid off real quick.

But inside that can is not cookies. Inside is little pieces of fur and material and thimbles and needles and thread and a Bible. And the kind of *ulu* Mom uses to cut meat, only smaller—too small for a big person to use on meat. I take that little *ulu* out and pretend I am a very little person, eating very little pieces of meat, rocking it back and forth on its rounded blade. This makes my stomach growl again, so I put the *ulu* down on my lap and dig underneath everything else in that can. Maybe there's still one little cookie left at the bottom. Even one little piece of a cookie. But no, it's only more scraps of fur and more pieces of material, cut in different kind of shapes. And way down at the very bottom, something else: one big blue bead. Blue like the kind of crayon they got at school, the one that says *cobalt*. One big cobalt blue bead.

I take it out and hold it. I like the way it feels in my hand, round and warm and hard as a stone.

I think of the story about the guy who finds a magic lamp and gets a wish by rubbing it. I rub the bead and try make a wish, but nothing happens. Thinking about wishes only makes me sad. My wishes feel like seagulls, flying off on screechy wings.

Suddenly there's a whispery sound down the hall, coming from Aaka's room, and I jump. The bead bounces right out of my hand and rolls across the floor.

How come I have to be so clumsy?

I hear Aaka now, and I don't think twice about what to do. I shove the lid back on the can quick and sit up straight. Never mind the bead.

I'm still holding the can on my lap when Aaka walks into the living room, her Eskimo slippers scratching across the floor.

Time to go beachcombing, Aaka says. She looks at me. Me, sitting there with that can on my lap, big as a basketball. But Aaka doesn't say anything about the can.

When she turns her back I shove it onto the table, fast, but when I lean over, the little *ulu* clatters to the hard floor with a metal slap. Dumb! How come I forgot to put it away? Aaka stops still, but she doesn't turn around. Doesn't even look at me.

You not supposed to pakak in other people's stuff, she says.

I look down, embarrassed.

Aaka stands by the window, watching the seagulls. *You put my sewing ulu back where it belongs and go get your brother out of bed. Time to go get clams.*

I pry the lid off the can and shove the ulu inside, quick as I can.

Kitta! Aaka says.

I could tell what *Kitta!* means by the way she says it. *Kitta!* means *Move it!* I move it right out of the room and down the hall, looking back real quick to see where that bead went. But all I see is Aaka's pictures, staring at me with their same faces, and Aaka, standing there, waiting.

Isaac is still half asleep and wants cereal, but Aaka hands us our jackets and shoos us out the door.

We gonna have to hurry, we gonna get clams, she says.

She makes us stick plastic grocery bags in our pockets and says to hurry so we could be first on the beach. Neither me or Isaac wants to be first anywhere, but we don't argue because you aren't supposed to argue with old people.

You two gonna like clams, she says. *They taste real good with seal oil.*

Outside is cold, way colder than in Anchorage where it's still summer, but I don't mind. Summer in Anchorage got bad breath, full of grease and car smoke and the sound of Stephan cussing. Fall in Aaka's village is full of the sound of seagulls and the clean cold breath of the wind.

The beach is littered with seaweed and driftwood and bits of shells and I like the way it smells, too. Like fish and something else I can't quite say. Something good I never smelled yet.

See the broken shells? Aaka says. We nod.

The same wind that shaked the house all night long throwed broken shells all across the beach. Clams. Clams pounded into the sand so hard they lying at the edge of the water like a mess of broken eggshells.

We walk along the beach picking up broken clams and putting them into our bags. The water swishes against the sand and the seagulls fly above us and Isaac keeps forgetting to pick up his clams, but Aaka never scolds. Isaac is looking at all the other stuff—all the different-colored rocks and bits of colored glass, smooth and round, and all the little pieces of pointy stick he could draw with in the sand. I stuff my bags full of clams. They smell just like the sea.

It takes a long time to pick all those clams clean of broken shells, all right, but they taste good, just like Aaka says, dipped in seal oil. Better than popcorn even. But Isaac wrinkles his nose and says no. He isn't hungry.

Isaac never eat seal oil before. Not like me. He only eat McDonald's. McDonald's and pizza. And Sailor Boy. He don't remember back to when Mom and me used to have seal oil all the time. Back before Stephan.

But I remember. I remember for both of us.

Nightmares

The people who come to Aaka's house all act like they know us, me and Isaac, even though they don't. And they all hug us hard every time, which makes me feel funny. I try pull away sometimes, but they don't let me. Some of the people talk mostly Iñupiaq, and some talk more English, real quiet, and some don't hardly talk at all, like my cousin, Iñuuraq, who is way older than me and gets to help Aaka cut meat.

Uncle comes on a four-wheeler after lunch. We watch him roar up the beach and park by the house. Isaac wants to go outside right away and get a ride. I want to go back into the bedroom and hide. I hate the sound of loud cars and loud four-wheelers.

Uncle been up the coast hunting, because fall is the time to find fat caribou. That's what Uncle says. And Uncle brought Aaka one.

Maybe you gonna go next time, Uncle tells Isaac and Isaac gets so excited he can't hardly stop jumping around the house, in and out of Aaka's rooms like a jack-in-the-box.

Uumaa! Aaka tells Uncle in a sharp voice. *Stop making the boy go wild.* But Uncle just laughs and messes Isaac's hairs, which makes him even wilder.

Uncle caught a caribou and now Aaka and Iñuuraq got its leg on the table, cutting up the meat, which is covered with white fat. My mom only gets caribou when somebody brings some to Anchorage in a bag, and then we always make caribou soup sometimes, which is my favorite. But I never seen a whole leg before, which is why I'm watching close. I want to know how to cut it. Aaka pokes the meat with her fingers, telling Iñuuraq what to do.

This part for roast, Aaka says, pinching the fattest part of the leg and drawing a line across it with her fingers. *And this one here for quaq.* She bends the meat where the bone's at so you could see the knee. *Cut it right here,* she says, poking at the knobby part. *And give these bones down here to your uncle to cut up for soup.*

Iñuuraq uses the *ulu* with strong hands, cutting at just the right spot to make it come apart. I'm itching to try, too, but I don't say it.

Could I help Uncle cut the bones? Isaac says. Isaac rocks his chair, excited, bumping me on the arm. My arm makes the *ulu* fall off the table. Aaka frowns.

Somebody gonna cut themselves, you don't quit jumping around, Aaka says.

I reach down to pick up the *ulu* and that's when I see the bead, Aaka's big blue bead. It rolled under the refrigerator and now it's just sitting there where nobody could see it— nobody but me.

But nobody's even looking, anyhow, not even Aaka, because everybody in the whole house is going outside to help Uncle with the rest of the caribou. Even Aaka. Everybody but me.

The bead is smudged with refrigerator dust and makes a greasy spot on my jeans when I pull it out and rub it clean. I hold it up to the light and squint into it. I like the way it looks with light coming through it, turning everything blue.

All of a sudden I know I'm not alone. Someone is standing in the doorway watching me play with that bead—and that someone is Aaka. The blood drains right out of my face and I want to quit breathing.

How come you don't go out with the others, Aaka says. She's looking right at the bead.

Why you wanna be in here all by yourself? she asks.

That's when I realize why Aaka act like she can't see the bead: Aaka's blind, or mostly blind. Part of me is relieved about this, but the other part is scared. I never even realized Aaka was almost blind. Never even guessed.

You quit moping around and go outside, Aaka says, and I do.

WE EAT fried meat for dinner, which is very good, especially the fat part. Fried meat with lots of fat makes me feel warm and sleepy. Aaka uses her meat to mop up the seal oil on her plate. Aaka puts seal oil on everything. I watch the way she uses her hands, not even looking down. Her hands don't make any mistakes, cutting her meat with an *ulu*.

Uncle eats his meat with little chunks of blubber called *qavsiraq,* which taste better than seal oil. Even Isaac likes *qavsiraq*, chewing with his mouth too full. *Qavsiraq* is Mom's favorite, too. That's what Uncle says.

Aarigaa! We gonna sleep good tonight, Uncle says, sprinkling little squares of *qavsiraq* onto our plates and smacking his lips.

Blessing don't hardly sleep at all sometimes, Isaac says. How does he know? I wonder. Then I remember him looking at me, wide-eyed in the middle of the night.

Uncle is watching me in a way that makes me itch.

How come you never sleep, Nutaaq? Nightmares?

Nightmares, Isaac agrees, his mouth full of meat.

You know how you get rid of nightmares? Uncle says.

I don't say anything.

How? Isaac asks.

You tell them your Iñupiaq name, Uncle says. *That's how you fix them kind. Nightmares are scared of Iñupiaqs.*

My name is Tupaaq, Isaac says, puffing up his chest.

Uncle smiles.

And Tupaaq was a very strong man, too, Uncle says. *Nightmares are really scared of Tupaaq.*

Isaac flexes his skinny little muscles and everybody laughs.

THAT NIGHT I fall asleep with the bead under my pillow. The bead I should have put back in Aaka's tin but didn't. I dream bad dreams about Stephan, but Uncle's right: Stephan is afraid of *Nutaaq.*

Nutaaq and her magic bead.

In the morning I wake up late, feeling happy. My cousin Iñuuraq is already here, eating Sailor Boy and jam.

Araa, your hair, Aaka says. *You never brush it yet.*

My hair is still all wrinkled up from my mom's braid and now the wrinkles have turned into tangles and the tangles are making lumps near the back of my neck.

My mom always braid it, I tell Aaka.

Aaka doesn't say anything.

You could try fix it yourself, Iñuuraq says.

I don't know how, not the way Mom does.

What grade you in?

Six.

You're big enough to fix your own hair, Iñuuraq says. *Come on. I show you.*

And she does, too. But the kind of braid she shows me is not the kind that goes round and round like a shiny crown. The kind of braid Iñuuraq makes goes straight down my back like a long black rope.

Ulu

Uncle made a new *ulu*, smaller than Aaka's. The handle is a piece of ivory polished smooth, and the blade looks like a whale's tail.

One of our aunties is holding Uncle's *ulu* up in the air, pretending to use it.

Just right for my hand, Auntie says.

Auntie's hand is small but chubby. The fat on Auntie's hand rolls over top of uncle's *ulu* like bread dough. Isaac giggles.

Isaac wants to hold the *ulu*, too, but he don't ask. Even Isaac knows that *ulus* are only for women. Big women, like Auntie, not kids like us.

Today's my birthday. Thanks, Cuz, Auntie says, smiling sweetly at Uncle and winking at me and Isaac. She waves the *ulu* back and forth with a look that says, *I jokes. It's not really my birthday.*

Uncle laughs. *Not for you*, he says, taking the *ulu* from Auntie.

Isaac is watching how Uncle sharpens the ulu. He uses a file and a stone, a round smooth stone, working it back and forth across the blade in slow even motions. I like to watch the way Uncle works, so careful, even with such a little thing. Uncle, who's big enough to wrestle the wind with one hand, is holding that tiny *ulu* with fingers as gentle as wings.

Could I try sharpen it? Isaac asks.

You gotta learn how first. These women are real picky about their ulus. Uncle winks at Isaac. The way he winks says Isaac knows all about women, which he don't. Isaac tries to wink back but blinks both eyes instead. Isaac don't know how to wink, either.

Uncle spends a lot of time sitting at Aaka's table, sharpening that *ulu*, while Aaka stands by the stove, frying caribou meat. The smell of that meat makes my mouth water. When Aaka puts the plates on the table, Uncle pulls his chair up close and looks at me.

Here, he says, handing me the *ulu*. *Try use it on your meat.*

I look at Aaka real quick, but Aaka isn't watching. Aaka isn't even hearing. I take the *ulu* and push it hard into the meat but nothing happens.

No, not that way, Auntie says, laughing. *That's not how Iñupiaqs do it. Here. Give it to me.*

I give Auntie the *ulu*, even though I don't want to, and I look down, my face burning. I don't like the way Auntie laughed at me. And I don't like the way she leans right over top of my plate and starts cutting my meat into little pieces, like I'm a baby.

This way, she says, popping chunks of meat into her mouth with fat little fingers. *You were holding it wrong.*

The way she does it makes it look easy, moving her wrist back and forth and making the round blade slice the meat, smooth as a spoon.

Now I see what I did wrong.

Then she lays the *ulu* down on my plate with a look that says, *You try.*

I feel my face get red, but I don't want anybody laughing at me anymore, so I pick up that *ulu*, like I been doing it ever since I was born, and I slice my meat just the way Auntie did it, smooth as butter, back and forth.

Auntie nods her head and smiles.

Uncle taps the *ulu* with one big finger. *Now you got your first present, and it isn't even your birthday*, Uncle says, grinning at Auntie.

My new *ulu* fits my hand just right and I hold it right, too, slicing meat like a real Iñupiaq, warm with happiness.

But all of a sudden I think about the bead in my pocket, Aaka's bead that I pretended was mine—the one I stole— and my happiness turns cold and hard.

September

In School

The waves are not pounding at the beach anymore. The waves have gotten too lazy to pound. The ocean is starting to freeze and the waves roll up and down real slow. The ocean is gray and icy, like a giant cup of slushie somebody's tilting back and forth. Pretty soon the ocean will freeze. That's what Aaka says.

First day of school I try braid my hair like Iñuuraq showed me. But I don't get it right, not like the way Mom does. I still have Aaka's bead in my pocket, too, where I can touch it with the tips of my fingers all day long. I pretend it's magic and could protect me from mean kids, the ones that always call you names and try fight sometimes. The ones that always pick on me.

The school in Aaka's village isn't hard to find. It's painted gray and bigger than everything else in the whole village, so no matter where you go, you can always look back and see it, peeking out from in between the houses like a big shadow.

Everyone goes to that one school, even Iñuuraq, who is almost too old for school. Iñuuraq doesn't go as early as me and Isaac, though, because she gets to go to the high school side of the school, which starts later.

All the kids in the elementary and middle school side walk to school together in big groups. Everyone except me and Isaac, who walk alone, a group of two. Two new kids.

A group of girls my age is walking next to us and I can see them, from the side of my eyes, looking at us real close the way people always look at strangers. Like they want to make fun of the way Isaac tries hold my hand when he sees them staring. I frown at Isaac, telling him, with my eyes, to act his age, and he frowns back, jutting his chin out to show how tough he is. The toughest six-year-old ever.

Who's your name? one of the girls calls out. I look over at the group to see who said it. She's staring right at me. She doesn't look like she's trying to be mean, but her eyes are suspicious.

Blessing, I tell her.

What kinda name's Blessing? another girl asks. That girl has a dirty face and mean eyes. *Blessing ain't no kind of Eskimo name,* she says. *Where you from?*

We're Eskimo, Isaac says, emphasizing the word *Eskimo.*

Yeah? So what's your Eskimo name? that girl asks me, imitating the way Isaac said it.

Nutaaq, I say, standing up tall and staring at that girl hard as I can, my hand on Isaac's shoulder. *And this one here is Tupaaq.*

That girl stares right back at me, too. But she doesn't say another word.

INSIDE THE SCHOOL you could forget where you are and think you're in Anchorage, because all the classrooms and offices look the same as in our school in Anchorage, only smaller. Even the bulletin boards look the same, with pictures of big trees and colored leaves, even though we don't have trees up here.

But the kids don't look the same. The kids are all Iñupiaq, just like me, so I'm not the only one in my class anymore, which is good. But they still look at me funny, like they're all part of the same family and I'm not, just like in Anchorage.

When I look out the window, though, it doesn't look anything like Anchorage. Outside the window is no trees, no cars, no McDonald's, and no stop signs. Only tundra, dark red and gold. And wind, which is blowing over the tundra grass and pressing it flat. The sun shines in some places and the clouds make shadows in other places. You could even see the shapes of the clouds in the shadows they make because there's no trees or buildings in the way to block them. The cloud shadows blow across the tundra like giant gray birds flying low.

There's a graveyard right outside the window, too, which is weird: a whole field of white crosses, growing up out of the tundra right next to the school like a forest of ghosts.

I think about ghosts and about this story Mom used to tell. Mom said there was a ghost that used to live in her *aaka*'s house. Mom said it wasn't a scary ghost, but it always scared me, all right. Those kind of stories always make me be afraid of the dark. And besides, the ghost in Mom's story was a baby, which is even scarier. Mom used to hear it crying, sometimes in the middle of the night. That's the part that scared me most. I look at those crosses, shining in the sunlight, and I shiver.

THE GIRL with the dirty face is called Sylvia and she's in my class. So are her friends, who all frown at me like they think I might try steal something. Those girls must be sisters or cousins because when the teacher reads names, they all have the same last name.

I don't have any sisters or cousins in this class—I don't have any friends here, either. Not like Sylvia.

Sylvia and her sister-cousins sit together, staring at me. I sit looking out the window at all the crosses, trying to pretend I can't see those girls. Trying to pretend it's only me and the crosses, all alone in the whole wide world.

When the teacher says my name, the sister-cousins giggle and suddenly I wish my *aaka* had never given me such a dumb name as Blessing. *Blessing.* Who ever heard of such a stupid name, anyhow?

But my new teacher, Miss Colato, does not think Blessing is dumb.

Blessing! What an unusual name, Miss Colato says.

Sylvia's gang giggles and looks at me, like they think Miss Colato is making fun of me. I glare back at them.

You must be a very special person to have such an unusual name, Miss Colato says.

I can't help it. I look over at Sylvia and smile a very *special* smile. She glares back.

Miss Colato is a very special teacher, too. That's what I

think. I like her, even if she uses words we don't hardly ever use, like *unusual*.

I like unusual words.

There's a lot of words in this world, in a lot of different languages, Miss Colato says, which is something I never really thought about before. Miss Colato is telling us about Spanish, which is her language. In Spanish, *sí* means yes and *no* means no.

How do you say yes and no in Iñupiaq? Miss Colato asks.

When Miss Colato says this, everybody gets real quiet, like they're afraid to say. Or don't want to. Then she tells us how some people make money translating words from one language to other languages and one of the girls says her auntie does that, too.

I know how to say yes and no in Iñupiaq. Mom taught me. I look at Sylvia and her sister-cousins, but I don't say anything. They'd probably laugh at how I say it.

There are different ways of talking English, too, Miss Colato is telling us. Like the kind they talk in Texas, which is called Southern English, and the kind we talk here in Alaska, which is called Village English. And the kind they talk in school, which is called School English. Different kinds of English are not good or bad. Just different.

That's what Miss Colato says.

We are going to learn how to translate Village English into School English.

If you want to drink somebody's Coke in Village English you say, *I uksi?*

If you want to drink somebody's Coke in School English you say, *May I have a sip, please?*

There's also manners. In school you say *please*. At home

we don't have to. At home it's rude to point. In school it's okay.

Sylvia is looking at me with a mean look.

Naumi. That's how you say no in Iñupiaq and *ii,* that's yes.

Ii, I like Miss Colato.

Naumi, I do not like mean girls.

HOW COME *your hair looks funny?* Sylvia asks, pointing at me. *Your braid's crooked,* she says.

We're walking home from school, me and Isaac, walking along the slushy beach with Sylvia, two girls, and one boy following. I pretend I never hear.

Who's your dad and mom then? Sylvia asks.

I never even look at her. The fact that we don't have a dad is none of her business.

Our mom is Rose, Isaac says, trying to sound tough.

So what's your mom's Iñupiaq name? Sylvia asks. She says that word *Iñupiaq* like she thinks I don't know what it means, but I do. *Iñupiaq* means *Real People,* that's what I know.

Isaac looks up at me, waiting for me to say Mom's Iñupiaq name, but I can't, because I don't know it. I never even thought about it before. Does Mom even have an Iñupiaq name? If she doesn't, does that mean we aren't real Iñupiaq? I look out over the water, avoiding Isaac's eyes, pretending I never heard what Sylvia asked. The sky is gray as gunmetal and the seagulls fly across it without a sound, like the sky's too heavy to hold their cries anymore.

The only other names I know for my mom are the bad ones Stephan uses.

I squeeze the bead in my pocket as hard as I can, pushing it against the bones in my hand until it hurts, like a bruise.

Isaac is still watching me, waiting for me to answer Sylvia's question. *What's your Iñupiaq name?* I want to ask her, but the way that one boy glares at us makes me turn away from Sylvia and smile hard at Isaac.

Race you home! I cry, running off toward Aaka's house, not even looking back at Sylvia and her crowd. Not even caring.

We race all the way home, me and Isaac, and I let Isaac win. Isaac is racing against me, but I'm racing against all these thoughts I don't want to be thinking. The thoughts race right along with me and they don't even stop running when I stop.

Why can't I even remember Mom's name, her real Iñupiaq name?

Eskimo Dancing

Aaka takes me to Eskimo dance practice. Before her eyes got bad Aaka used to dance, too. Now she only listens. I don't want to go at all, not even just to listen, because dancing is evil. If you start dancing, you gonna dance yourself right to hell. That's what Pastor Sellers used to say, because the devil gets inside you when you dance. Right inside. I don't even want to go into the room where they dance, but Aaka makes me.

Aaka's embarrassed that I don't want to watch the dancers, but I don't care. I do not want the devil inside me. Aaka could make me go in the room, all right, but she can't make me watch. I sit next to Aaka and when she puts her hand on my shoulder, I slouch down and pull my sweatshirt hood over my eyes.

Uumaa! What's wrong with you? Aaka says.

I peek out from under my hood. Sylvia is one of the

dancers and she's wearing a new Eskimo dress, the kind with a hood and a skirt. And her face is not dirty, either. She looks very different from how she looks at school. Sylvia, the devil-dancer, who pretends she can't see me. Me, sitting next to Aaka and wishing I was somewhere else.

When the drumming starts, it shakes the whole room like an earthquake and makes my heart jump into my throat so fast I feel sick. The drumbeats swell inside my chest, pounding straight through my whole body, shaking everything upside down. Marching me right off to hell.

Then the voices start to sing. The men's voices, deep like drums, and the women's, flying over top like birds. Soaring. I can't understand the meaning of the words, but they're strong words, not evil words. I close my eyes and try feel what they mean.

Yungy, yungy yung, the words say, proud and happy-sounding.

Two of the men are dancing all by themselves, and I don't mean to watch them but I can't help it. The way those men dance makes me forget about the drummers drumming and the singers singing. It's like the dancing and the drumming and the singing are all one thing, one very big thing. Like a mountain, which isn't a good thing or bad thing, but just is.

When they stamp their feet, the drums pound louder and the voices rise higher and it makes me want to jump up and dance with them. My foot even moves, all by itself, trying to stamp, which scares me. Is there a force stronger than me making me want to dance even though I know it's evil? I think about how it would feel to have the devil inside, forcing me to dance, making me stomp and stomp and stomp, all the way to hell.

Part of me wants to hide my eyes with my hood, all right, but another part wants to keep on watching the way those men dance. And bit by bit, that part is winning.

They move together, like they're attached to each other by the sound, those men. And when they hold their arms out in a certain way, their arms turn into walrus tusks and the men turn into walruses. You could see them dive and rise along with the music. They dance a strong walrus dance with their tusks out, lifting their legs and stamping their feet and crying *Uiiii?* in voices that turn up at the end, like a question. Like they want to know if we agree with them. Without even thinking, I raise my eyebrows to say *Ii,* I agree. I really do. Pretty soon I'm not even hearing the beating of the drums at all anymore. It's inside my chest now, like my own heartbeat. Like my own heart has grown big as the world.

Suddenly I know what I want. More than anything, I want to dance like those men.

When the dancing is over, Aaka is talking away in Iñu-piaq to the other old people and the drummers are putting away their drums. Sylvia brushes past me without even looking. She's wearing fancy boots with black and white fur trim and she acts like she's the best dancer in the world, better than everyone. Suddenly I am very, very sure that I am gonna learn to dance—and I'll dance better than Sylvia.

THAT NIGHT me and Isaac try dance in our room before we go bed, stamping our feet hard and crying *Uiiii!* We forget how loud we are and we don't even notice how Aaka is standing there at the door, watching us stamp around the room. We don't even see her until we flop onto the bed, all worn out.

Girls don't stamp their feet that way, Aaka says. *Only boys dance like that.*

As soon as she says it I know it's true, because I remember how Sylvia and the other women were swaying, not stamping. This makes me mad. How come girls don't get to stamp their feet?

Like this, Aaka says, swaying back and forth with her head down and her arms up high, patting the air like there's an invisible drum. The way Aaka does it, you could just about hear that drum pounding.

After Aaka leaves and Isaac falls asleep I try, too, swaying back and forth real quiet, to the sound of a pretend drum. My pretend drum beats every time I move my arms and pretty soon it isn't even pretend anymore. Pretty soon I could even hear drumbeats in the sound of wind, like the wind knows I'm dancing, and the wind agrees.

Uiiii! the wind cries.

I imagine myself wearing fancy boots, like Sylvia's, the kind Aaka calls Eskimo boots. My hair is braided all the way around my head, like a crown, and I know all the moves and never make one mistake. I dance so perfect Sylvia has to follow me. This is what I imagine—me in front and Sylvia in back trying real hard to follow my perfect dance. But I am too fast for Sylvia. *Too fast.*

Then I remember how real Iñupiaqs aren't supposed to brag and how Pastor Sellers said dancing is evil. And how Sylvia asked my mom's Iñupiaq name and I didn't even know it.

Does she even have one?

And if my mom doesn't have an Iñupiaq name, how she gonna keep nightmares away? I don't want to think about this, wide awake in Aaka's dark house, but I can't help it. Outside, I hear the sound of the wind blowing. It sounds like a lonely woman, way far off, moaning and crying.

Nukaaluga

Aaka is sewing and I like watching her, because Aaka concentrates hard when she sews, like sewing is the only thing in the whole world. I like the way her hand flies, fast as a bird—machine-fast in and out, her stitches straight as staples. Aaka's hands know exactly what to do, all by themselves, without her eyes even watching. Like her hands have their own eyes. She sits on the floor, one leg under her butt, the other straight out in front, the TV making noise in the corner, where Isaac's watching his cartoons.

Aaka's making a brand-new parka for Isaac out of sealskin.

Thread my needle, Nukaaluga, she says, handing it to me.

I don't ask what *nukaaluga* means; I take a spool of thread from the table and start threading the needle. Maybe *nukaaluga* means *granddaughter.* I pull the thread out straight and hand it back. Aaka checks it with her fingers.

No, not that thread. Use the other one.

I look around, but I don't see no other.

We got more. Go get that one on the table by my bed.

I never been in Aaka's bedroom before. Aaka told us not to *pakak* there but now she wants me to. The room scares me. It's small and dark with a little bed and the curtains are closed. When I turn on the light switch, the light don't come on. I guess maybe the light burnt out and Aaka never changed it because she don't see good enough to need it.

I stick my hand in my pocket and hold on tight to the bead. Standing in a dark room thinking about Aaka's blindness scares me.

Bit by bit my eyes get used to the dark room and finally I see the thread, sitting on the table by her bed, right next to an old picture in a dusty gold frame. My eyes open wide when I see that picture. I pick it up and look real close just to make sure. It's the same one my mom had before it got broke, a brownish picture of my great-grandma Nutaaq and my great-grandpa Tupaaq both wearing old-style fur parkas long time ago, when they were young. My great-grandma's parka is very fancy, with little tufts of fur on the shoulders and a big fat ruff. It got pretty designs around the bottom, too, and white fur sewn on the front to look like walrus tusks. My great-grandpa is very big and my great-grandma is very small and very beautiful, too. Both of them are almost smiling and almost sad, too.

I think about my mom and about this person she called Mom—Nutaaq, her grandma—the Nutaaq in this picture. Then I think about how Aaka has this picture on a table in a dark room where she can't even see it and how my mom is all alone in Anchorage where *her* picture got broken. Standing alone in Aaka's dark room thinking all these things makes my chest get tight, so I close my eyes and try make my brain stop thinking so much. But even with my eyes closed I still see that same picture, with both of my great-grandparents smiling, lying on the floor of our apartment in Anchorage, broken.

I wonder if they let Mom take that picture with her to treatment. What if they never? What if they left that picture lying on the floor and what if somebody came in and swept it up and threw it out with the trash?

I think about my mom, all alone in treatment with a broken arm and no kids and not even her favorite picture left to remind her of her family.

Then I grab the thread and get out of Aaka's bedroom fast, shutting the door behind me.

I want to shut the door to my thoughts, too, but I can't.

Aaka shows me how to take the new thread, which looks more like string, and pull it into pieces skinny enough to thread into a needle. Aaka has cut out little pieces of sealskin so I could try sew, too.

You could sew a yo-yo, she says. *An Eskimo yo-yo.*

She shows me how to make the stitches, in and out, straight as staples. The way she does it makes it look easy, but when I try, my stitches keep trying to get big and go crooked and the seam gets full of bumps. When I finish, Aaka feels the bumps with her fingers and says, *No. Not like that.* Then she takes her *ulu* and cuts through my stitches— *rip, rip, rip*—just like that. Without a word.

Looking at all those little broken threads that used to be my stitches makes me want to cry. I feel embarrassed, and mad, too. So mad I want to get up and run right outside, run away from Aaka and her sharp little *ulu.*

Here, Aaka says. *Like this.* She sews a few little stitches into it on each side and hands it back to me with a look that says, *Here, you try,* but I don't. I just sit there, looking at Aaka.

Aaka looks right back and says, *First time I tried sew a parka I got the back so crooked it was hanging down lower than the rest, real funny-looking. My brother sure laughed. He said I'd sewed myself a tail.*

Aaka smiles. I smile, too, thinking about Aaka with a tail.

Boy, did I feel bad that time, Aaka says. *But Mom said never mind. She ripped it apart and let me try again.* Aaka nods at my yo-yo, her own needle and thread midair. *Sew it back up and never mind. It's gonna get better.*

Aaka's wrong. That's what I think. Sewing is never gonna get better. Sewing is too hard. But this time my seam doesn't get so bumpy. After I finish one part I hand it to Aaka to check. She runs her finger over my stitches and I hold my breath, eyeing her *ulu.*

Not bad, she says, handing it back. *Now finish it.*

I let out my breath and smile, without even thinking.

I work on finishing my yo-yo and Aaka works on Isaac's parka and we don't talk anymore because we don't have to. And besides, I'm trying too hard to keep my stitches straight to talk. The thimble Aaka made me use keeps getting in the way and the thread gets greasy and slippery. But after a while the sewing really does start to get easier and I start thinking about Aaka's dark room and what I saw there.

We got that same picture, I say all of a sudden. The words make my throat feel itchy because I didn't mean to say them. Not out loud.

Aaka looks up and frowns for a second like she's trying to see my words floating somewhere in the air in front of her

October

Telling Stories

The snow is falling and it's dark and cold when we go school and dark when we get home and scary dark when we go bed, sometimes. We watch out the window at school while the sun comes up and goes right back down. Like it's scared of the dark, too. When we get out of school the moon is already shining on the snow and the dark sky is glittering with stars before dinner, even.

I'm not used to so much dark. Dark and wind, dark and wind, from the time we get up until the time we go bed. And I have to put Isaac to bed even when he don't want to go, because Aaka says I'm Big Sister.

Isaac, who always try act like he's too big to go bed when I say. Too big to do anything he don't want to.

Tell me a story, he says, and I do because I'm good at stories. Just like Mom.

I know how to change things in stories to make them fit better, too, like how to turn the lemming story Mom used to tell into a stay-in-bed-Isaac story. The lemming could be a little boy tucked under an *E.T.* blanket, a little boy who says he's too big for bed.

I'M BIG! the little boy roars, his head buried in his blanket. *TOO BIG FOR BED!*

I lean over him, talking slow in my spooky Magic Woman voice.

You are not so big. You are just a silly little lemming.

I'm not a lemming! he says, making gun sounds with his mouth. *I'M BIG. BIGGER THAN THE BIGGEST THING.*

What is the biggest thing, little lemming?

But Isaac, he don't even listen, he just says over and over: *Bigger than the biggest thi-ing, bigger than the biggest thi-ing.* Because that's the way boy lemmings are; they like to make noise with their mouths and try act like they're the biggest.

There is no such thing as the biggest thing, Magic Woman whispers. *There's always something bigger than the biggest thing.*

No way, Boy Lemming says. *I'm bigger, I am bigger than the whole wide world!*

The sun's bigger than the world, Magic Woman says. *Jupiter is bigger.*

My head tips over Jupiter, my foot stamps out the sun.

Magic Woman swoops down, quick as an owl, catching that silly little Boy Lemming in her net.

You're not so big, she says, pinning him underneath his *E.T.* blanket-net. *And you'd better stay in bed, too! Stay under the blanket, you silly little lemming. It's safer.*

Isaac giggles and kicks at the blanket, but I'm bigger, so he's stuck.

Finally, in his toughest voice, he shouts, *Let me out, I am not a lemming! I'm Tupaaq!*

And I let him out as soon as he says it, too, because a name is powerful, just like Aaka said.

Aaka was listening to the story, too. I could tell by her face when I go back to the kitchen to get water.

My dad used to tell that lemming story, she says quietly.

I learned it from my mom, I say.

And she learned it from her grandma Nutaaq. Nutaaq was a good storyteller, too, just like you, Nukaaluga.

Her words make me swell with pride. I am good with stories, just like mom. Just like my great-grandma Nutaaq, the storyteller.

I think about this one story, the way Mom told it to me and Isaac and the way Aaka's mom probably told it to her. I bet Aaka never heard it the way I told it to Isaac. Then I think about how stories can change, just like how people change. Just like how it seems Aaka has changed from when we first came, and how Isaac has changed, too, and isn't a baby anymore.

And what about me? Have I changed? I don't know.

But when I tell Aaka about how stories change, she says no, stories don't change. They grow in people's hearts, just like people grow. Stories say different things at different times, but they don't change. That's what Aaka says.

Tavra.

That's what storytellers say at the end of the story.

Tavra.

That's all.

Quyanaq

You see my scissors? Aaka says. Aaka's always looking for things when she sews sometimes.

My old eyes, they like frosty windows. Can't see out, sometimes, only in. That's what Aaka says.

I've been thinking about this for a while now, wondering how the world looks when you're almost blind. Like big shadows moving outside a window, maybe. But when Aaka sews, she needs to see little things, too, like needles and thimbles and thread.

I could be your eyes, I tell Aaka.

Aaka says, *Okay, Nukaaluga, you be Aaka's eyes. You find my scissors.*

I find them on a little table next to a piece of caribou antler and a picture of Uncle in a white parka, sitting in the snow. I bring the scissors to Aaka and she reaches out for them without looking, feeling in my hand for them.

Quyanaq, Aaka says. *Quyanaqpak.*

That's how you say *thank you* in Iñupiaq, *thank you very much*. I didn't know this before, but I do now.

Outside is dark and cold these days, but inside is light and warm and it feels peaceful, sitting here where the wind can't come, sewing with Aaka. I'm making a string for my Eskimo yo-yo out of Aaka's special thread, the kind they make from caribou sinew. My yo-yo looks like two little drums, trimmed with white polar bear fur all around the edge. The fur sticks out straight on the sides the way little kids draw the sun. Now all I got to do is tie the yo-yos together so I could make them go round and round over top of my head like Uncle does. But I need something for the middle of the yo-yo string, something to hold on to when I swing it.

Dig in my sewing tin, Aaka says. *Maybe you gonna find something.*

Suddenly I remember the bead. Every drop of blood drains right out of my face.

Aaka wants me to find that bead. I know it. I could dig it out of my pocket quick and give it to her, but all of a sudden I can't move. Can't even breathe.

Aaka looks up.

Here. I find it, she says, sliding the tin off the table. Then she pulls the lid off and starts digging—digging and digging for that bead, which she can't ever find, because I got it in my pocket, heavy as lead. The bead I stole.

Now where that thing go? Aaka says.

Even though she isn't looking at me, it feels like she is. I want to tell her how I took the bead and didn't mean to keep it. I want to say that the bead got some kind of magic that wouldn't let me put it back. But my chest feels so tight I could hardly breathe. If I try talk, I might start crying.

Then I do cry.

At first I'm crying because I feel bad about the bead. Then, suddenly, I'm crying for everything else—Stephan cussing and Mom getting her arm broke and me getting a black eye and Isaac too little to understand anything and us not ever having a real family and kids like Sylvia saying we're not real Iñupiaq, either. And a whole bunch of other things that don't even got names. I cry so hard I'm gasping for breath like a fish that fell out of its tank.

It feels like all the tears that been stuck inside me since last summer are finally coming out. Like the tear faucet got turned on and wedged wide open.

Aaka puts her arm around me without saying anything and holds me until I start to get quiet.

It's okay, she says.

No, it's not, I sputter. *I took that bead. I took it!*

Aaka looks like she never even heard me and it suddenly becomes really, really important that I make her understand exactly what I did.

I took the bead out of your sewing tin without even asking!

Aaka's holding my head and stroking my hair. Now she stops and looks up into the empty air, as if she's trying to see what I'm saying.

Bead? she says.

I pull the bead out of my pocket, along with all the bits of pocket gunk, and give it to her. Aaka rolls it back and forth in her fingers.

Ah! she says, holding it in her two hands like that bead is warming her fingers. *My mom's bead, the one Aunt Aaluk gave her.*

The bead glows like a little blue lightbulb in her fingers and I am thinking about my great-great-aunt Aaluk, who went away and left this bead behind. And about my great-grandma Nutaaq, the one I'm named for.

Worth a lot them days, Aaka says, rolling the bead in her fingers. *A person could buy a boat back then with one of these beads. Or a sled and dogs. My mom had two beads, but this is the only one she kept.*

Two?

Aaka raises her eyebrows to say yes.

What happened to the other one?

Aaka gets real quiet and I think maybe she never hear me. She just sits there, holding that one bead up to the light, right in front of her eyes like she could see stories inside it.

The other one? she says, finally. *Oh. They bury that one with a baby that died in the Sickness that time, died with all those others.*

I think about a baby dying and about the crosses at the cemetery by the school and about the ghost baby that used to cry in that house where Mom's *aaka* lived, and I shiver like a gust of wind suddenly came right inside the house.

They think those beads have power, that time. That's how they used to think. That you could chase death away with one little bead.

Aaka shrugs.

I want to ask if we still think like that, but the way Aaka says it makes me know we don't.

Who was the baby? I ask.

Manu, Aaka says. *The baby's name was Manu, same as your mom.*

Manu!

All of a sudden I remember. *Manu*—that's my mom's

name, all right, her real Iñupiaq name. I knew it all along. I don't know how, but I did. Maybe I heard it when I was a baby, sitting on my mom's lap. Maybe I heard it when somebody took that picture of us two smiling. Maybe somebody said my mom's Iñupiaq name, real sweet, just to make her smile that way.

Manu.

Nutaaq, she sure loved that baby, Aaka says. *That's how come she give your mom that name—Manu.*

I fiddle with the strings of my new yo-yo, not knowing what else to say. Thinking about that baby that my mom was named after makes me feel sad and happy, both.

Suddenly, Aaka does a strange thing. She takes that bead and presses it gently into my hand, closing my fingers over top of it with both her hands. Aaka's hands feel cool and fluttery, like small brown birds about to fly. Then she digs into her sewing tin again, and pulls out a piece of her special thread.

You put the bead on this one, Nukaaluga, and wear it around your neck so it don't get lost. This one's Nutaaq's bead, all right. The one she kept to remember her sister by. Her sister, Aaluk.

I thread the bead through the string and look down at it, suddenly shy about putting it on.

Aaka's name is Aaluk, too, that's what I'm thinking. And this is the bead Aaluk gave to her sister, Nutaaq. Nutaaq just like me.

I look down at my yo-yo, still sitting on the table, still waiting for someone to put a holder on its string.

But I thought the bead was for the yo-yo, I say.

Aaka laughs. *That what you think?*

I nod.

Too small, Aaka says. *That yo-yo needs something bigger. Needs a piece of caribou antler like the kind I got somewhere. That one's gonna be just right if I could find it. Maybe we going to have to let your uncle cut a new one.*

That's when I remember the picture of Uncle, on the table, by the antler.

It's okay. I know where that antler is, I tell Aaka.

I go back to the little table, and the antler is still sitting there, right by the picture of Uncle wearing his hunting parka in the snow, laughing.

I put my hand to my chest and feel the bead—*my bead.*

Quyanaq, I think. *Quyanaqpak.*

Then I think about my great-grandma Nutaaq, and about the baby who died, the one that my mom got named after, and I feel the lump of tears in my chest, like there's still things that need to be cried about. But when I look at Uncle's smiling face I suddenly feel like laughing. Laughing and crying, both.

Some things are sad and happy and funny, all rolled up into one. That's what I think.

Dance Practice

I am not afraid of dancing anymore. The pastor at Aaka's church does not say dancing is evil, and she is way older than Pastor Sellers, so Aaka says she knows more. Me, too. I say she knows more, too. Besides, Aaka's pastor smiles nice and calls me Sweetie. Pastor Sellers never called me Sweetie.

I can dance now. I practice alone sometimes, when nobody sees, remembering how the women do it, moving my arms just like they do. I ask Aaka if I could try dance with the dancers and she says she's gonna ask if I could be in the dance group. Sylvia's gonna be mad, all right, but she can get as mad as she wants and it won't make any difference. Aaka is way older than Sylvia and you have to listen to your elders. That's what Uncle says. Even Uncle, who's way bigger than anyone, has to listen to *his* elder, which is Aaka. Besides, my mom has an Iñupiaq name and now I know what it is, so Sylvia can't tease me about it anymore.

When we walk into dance practice, Sylvia glares at me. I give Sylvia a *Ha ha* look, then turn away.

Come over here by the girls, one of the ladies says. *You stand right here and follow this girl in front of you.*

The girl in front of me is Sylvia, who turns around when I stand there, giving me a mean look nobody else could see. Sylvia's look says, *I'm too good and too fast for you to follow, ha ha.* I put my chin up and look right back at her.

Just watch me. That's what my look says.

But Sylvia can't watch, because she's in front of me, trying to turn her back to keep me from seeing how she moves. But I could see the other girls, all right. Sylvia can't stop me from watching how the others move. I follow how they put their feet and move their arms and bend their heads, swaying to the sound of the drums and the voices. The voices that make me think of birds, way up high on the wind.

Boom, boom, boom, the drums go. The sound makes my heart pound hard, too. *Boom. Boom. Boom.*

Yungy, yungy yah, the women sing, and it feels like the words are inside me, making me move the way they say, even though I don't know what they mean.

The drums and the singing are using me to tell a story, and if I close my eyes and block out everything else I could even understand the story. I couldn't say it out loud in words, but I feel it way down deep inside.

Boom, boom, boom.

Before I have a chance to think about it, I'm dancing, really dancing. Without even looking at the others, I'm dancing. Letting the drums and the voices tell me what to do and how to move. Dancing just right.

Even after the music stops, I still feel the dance, beating

inside my chest, like wings, and I stand there in the center of the room, happy. So happy I could almost forget about Sylvia and all her mean looks.

Who teach you to dance? one of the old men asks.

All of a sudden everybody is looking at me and everybody's eyes are saying the same thing: *Who teach you?*

Nobody, I whisper, suddenly afraid. Did I do it wrong? Was it bad the way I did it?

Then I see Sylvia's face and I know the truth. I danced good. Just as good as Sylvia.

Next it's the boys' turn to dance and I go sit in back with the other girls and the women and I don't even feel bad about the fact that I can't sing the words the way they can. Besides, the old lady next to me is singing loud enough for both of us, loud enough to break glass, just like in the cartoons. Thinking about this makes me smile and all of a sudden I want to hug her. I don't know why. I just do.

Dance practice is like that, I guess.

I think maybe that old woman could tell what I'm thinking, too, because after the dance is over, she leans down and puts her arm around me. But then, all of a sudden, she straightens up and looks at me surprised.

Where you get that bead? she asks.

That's when I realize that the bead, which I usually keep hidden, is not hidden anymore. It's hanging right over top of my shirt, plain as day.

My aaka give it to me.

That old woman looks at Aaka and Aaka says, *Nutaaq's bead,* and both of them nod like it's part of some story they both know.

I remember that bead, one of the old men says.

Aaka puts her hand on my shoulder and says, *Nutaaq*, and all the old people nod and smile like that explains everything.

I thought they buried that bead with Rose's aaka, one of the younger women says. All of a sudden everyone gets real quiet and Aaka has a look on her face that says, *Mind your own business*. But she doesn't say it.

I think that woman is about the same age as my mom. She has straight black hair with one yellow-orange streak and curly bangs. Now everyone's looking at her like she said something she shouldn't, but she just shrugs and starts helping the others put stuff away. Dance practice is over.

WHY YOU fighting with that girl? Aaka asks.

Aaka's making tea. Uncle is carving the caribou antler I found to make it right for my yo-yo handle. I don't have to ask Aaka what girl she's talking about because I already know.

Sylvia.

What I can't figure out is how Aaka could tell about me and Sylvia fighting. Aaka is almost blind and me and Sylvia never said a word.

I never, I say.

Aaka stirs her tea slowly, looking out the window like she isn't even listening. Outside you could see the beach in the dark. The ocean is covered with snowy ice.

You aren't supposed be like that when you dance.

Aaka doesn't say anything else. Me neither. But now I'm feeling guilty. Which makes me get even madder at Sylvia. Mean Sylvia and her whole big mean family of sister-cousins. Making me be mad, when I don't even want to be.

Then I think about that lady with the streak in her hair who thought my bead got buried with my great-grandma.

How come that lady thought the bead got buried? I ask Aaka.

Aaka doesn't ask what lady. Aaka knows. But her mouth gets tight like she don't want to talk about it.

That's what your mom wanted, Aaka says. *She wanted that bead to stay with her grandma Nutaaq, when Nutaaq died.*

I don't say anything. The refrigerator starts buzzing in the kitchen, very loud.

Mom wanted to chase death away, right, Aaka? Isaac says.

Aaka and I both look at Isaac, surprised. I didn't even know Isaac was listening and I sure didn't think he would understand what we were talking about, even if he did listen. But little kids are like that. They understand stuff nobody thinks they can. And they remember things, too. Things you thought they never even understood in the first place.

That's right, Aaka says, nodding at Isaac like she's talking to a grown-up. *That's what your mom wanted, all right, but that's not what* my *mom wanted. My mom, Nutaaq, she wanted that bead to stay with the others.*

What others? Isaac asks.

The ones your great-great-aunt Aaluk promised to bring her. Aaluk said when she comes back home, she gonna bring one bead for every person in our family.

I think of all of Aaka's family pictures, all those faces. One bead for each face? That's a lot of beads.

Where are the other beads? Isaac asks.

Aaka turns away. *Aaluk never come back,* she says.

Aaka is standing with her back to us, watching out the window where it's too dark to see. My *aaka* Aaluk. I put my hand up to my neck to feel the bead, Nutaaq's bead, the one she was given to remember her sister, Aaluk, by. But Aaluk left, just like we left Anchorage, and she never came back.

Back from where? Isaac says.

Aaka looks out the window, out across the frozen ocean.

She went over to the Russian side, Aaka says. I follow her eyes out across the ocean ice, wondering about the Russian side. I never thought about the ocean as having sides before.

I think about how far it must be, all the way across the ocean to the Russian side. Too far to walk, that's for sure, even if the ocean is frozen. Then I think about how far it is to Anchorage, even in a plane, flying all the way across the wide empty tundra, over the sharp white mountains, past the long loopy rivers. A person could never walk that far.

Why can't she fly back? I ask.

They don't let her, Aaka says.

Who? Isaac says.

The Russians.

How come?

Aaka looks at me and Isaac with a look that says, *Araa, quit asking so much questions, you two!*

Border's closed, she says.

I look out the window, trying to imagine a closed border, with my great-great-aunt all alone on the other side of it. Light flakes of snow are falling—sparkly specks in the dark sky—and I'm trying to imagine a fence out there somewhere in the darkness, a big frozen fence, wide as the ocean and shut tight. With people on the other side who can't get out.

Is a border some kind of fence?

No, Aaka says. *The border is not a fence. The border's just a line, somewhere out there in the ocean. It's just a line nobody could see and people can't cross it or they gonna get shot.*

But how could people know if they're crossing the border if nobody could see it? That's what I want to know.

Aaka's still looking out the window, still staring at the ice in the darkness, as if she could see something there.

My mom, Nutaaq, she always used to stand on the beach down there. Just looking. Crying, too, sometimes, real quiet. Missing her sister, Aaluk, more and more the older she gets.

I look out the window to where Aaka is looking— an empty patch of dark beach. I try to imagine my great-grandma Nutaaq, the one I'm named for, standing there on that spot, all alone, missing her sister who is stuck on the other side of the ocean, locked up behind a frozen border, way far away. Then I think of my mom, locked up on the other side of those sharp white mountain peaks we flew over, and I know how my great-grandma must have felt. I know exactly.

Aaka turns around and looks right at me, like she could suddenly see every little detail about me. *And they said Aaluk was very pretty, too, just like you,* Aaka says.

My face gets warm with embarrassment. Nobody ever called me pretty before.

Long shiny hair, just like you, and a tattoo on her chin like the kind they always have in the old days. Aaka smiles, just a little. *My mom, she sure always wanted a tattoo like that.*

My hand goes up to my chin and I think about my great-grandma missing her sister. Then I think about Sylvia and her sister-cousins and how it is to be jealous for all the things you never had and to miss all the things you lost. And somehow these two things feel all knotted up together inside until I can't tell anymore where one stops and the other starts.

Blessing's Bead

Uncle is carving the caribou horn to look just like a hand. Uncle could carve things all kinds of ways. He could make a little piece of ivory look just like a seal or a little man, dancing. And he could make a little piece of caribou horn look just like a hand with two fingers that make a V.

Blessing's got a yo-yo now, Uncle says, tying the string into the middle of the V and showing us how to swing it. He stretches his arm out and swings the yo-yo up and down until both strings start flying round and round like helicopter blades. He swings it all around on both sides and even over top of his head.

I try swing it that way, too, but at first the strings just get tangled up and the yo-yo won't fly.

I practice and practice until I get it right.

Aarigaa, Aaka says. *You getting pretty good with that thing.*

Aaka is watching—watching with her ears. She can hear

the *whir whir* of my yo-yo making perfect circles in the air. Backward, forward, and upside down.

I hold on tight to the yo-yo, making those little sealskin drums fly like birds, their tufts of polar bear fur waving over top of my head. And I could feel the bead, too, bumping against the bone in my chest every time I swing the yo-yo.

Nutaaq's bead. Nutaaq's bead and now mine, too, because I'm Nutaaq, Nutaaq and Blessing both.

I swing the yo-yo harder and harder and faster and faster until that is all there is: one Eskimo yo-yo making Aaka's whole house whir and one blue bead, bouncing against my chest.

Blessing's bead.

Iron Curtain

The sun is gone now. Even in the middle of the day it's only gray out. Dark gray like just after the sun first goes down. I sit in school, looking out the window at the crosses, which are almost invisible in the gray light. I'd rather look at ghost crosses than at real girls like Sylvia who act like they're better just because they got lots of cousins in this class.

Miss Colato has finished teaching about capitalization and now she's doing social studies.

Something Very Important has Happened to the World. Miss Colato says, as if she's capitalizing all the words she wants us to hear. *They've Opened the Iron Curtain!*

The Iron Curtain is in the middle of a big city in Germany and the people living on one side of it don't ever get to see the people on the other side, not even if they're brothers and sisters. That's what Miss Colato says.

They're separated, just like my great-grandma, the one I'm named after, and her sister, Aaluk.

But the Iron Curtain is not really a curtain and it isn't made out of iron, either. It's a wall made out of rock which keeps people away from each other. We get to see pictures of them pulling it down.

It's almost Thanksgiving and Miss Colato says we have a lot of things to be thankful for, like the Iron Curtain opening and like our moms and dads taking care of us. She says to draw a picture of something we feel thankful for and write about it.

I draw a picture of people opening a curtain and two women hugging each other. One of the women is my *aaka*'s mom, Nutaaq, and the other is Nutaaq's sister, Aaluk.

That's a dumb picture, Sylvia says. Sylvia who always think she knows everything and always try pick fights.

Real Iñupiaqs don't fight. That's what Aaka says. Then I think about Mom and Stephan fighting when they drink.

Real Iñupiaqs don't drink, either, I think. But what does that mean about Mom?

I crumple up my dumb picture and throw it away inside my desk.

Inside Out

Outside the church on Thanksgiving Day are boxes and boxes full of frozen whale meat and *maktak*, all cut up into fat chunks. Outside is dark like night, even though it's only noon. White sparkly snow is glittering in the dark, dark sky. And now it's blowing around our feet, too, like somebody smoking. Like the ground is smoking cold smokes.

Inside the church is cold, too, but not for me. Aaka make me fur boots, warm as mittens. Iñupiaqs call fur boots *kamaak*. That's what Uncle says.

We sit on a bench, me and Isaac and Aaka. We sit by Aaka's food box, waiting for them to bring the food in. Lots of other people come in and sit around us, sit on every bench and chair in every corner, and pretty soon the whole church is full of people. Everybody waiting with their own boxes.

Then the church gets warm even for people who aren't wearing *kamaak*.

In school, when Miss Colato said to write about what

we're thankful for and I crumpled up my picture of the Iron Curtain, I couldn't think of anything to write so I copied what Sylvia wrote: *I am thankful for my family.*

The family Sylvia drew had a mom and a dad, smiling big. Mine doesn't. Mine only has us three: old Aaka with her blind eyes, and Isaac, a big boy who still sucks his thumb sometimes, and me, a girl with a long braid and one blue bead. Some kind of family.

But inside the church at the Thanksgiving Day feast is so many people you can't even tell which are families and which aren't. Everybody's bunched up together like one big family. Babies are crying in their moms' parkas and old people are squawking from wheelchairs and bunches of kids of all sizes are playing everywhere. Big kids like my cousin Iñuu-raq are passing out foods and kids my age are pouring tea and coffee and little kids run around in circles making noise until Uncle says: *You kids go sit with your parents!* And everyone listens, even the ones who aren't with parents, because Uncle is big as a whale and his voice is even bigger. But his smile is big, too. His smile is so big it makes his eyes shut tight so he don't even see how some kids are still crawling around under the benches, folding church paper into paper airplanes.

THIS IS HOW they do Thanksgiving at my *aaka*'s village: First they give everybody all kinds of soups—duck soup and *niġliq* soup and caribou soup. Even chicken soup. Then they give everybody *quaq*—which is frozen whale meat and *maktak* and fish. Then Aaka cuts the *quaq* with her *ulu*, and me and Isaac puts salt on it. I cut my own *maktak* with my own *ulu*, which Uncle made me. The *maktak* is pink and black and it tastes smooth and good: cold on the way down but warm inside.

Then Uncle tells everybody how lucky we are to have this Thanksgiving feast in this church where we can all be together to celebrate the whales, because in other places they only have turkey all alone in their own apartments.

That's how it was in Anchorage, too, people always eat turkey on Thanksgiving, only my mom never have money to buy turkey, so we never. And I don't care, anyhow, because turkey is dry and tastes like grass. Turkey is not as good as *maktak*.

No way.

At the end of Thanksgiving they give everybody rice pudding and fruit and then everybody sings songs and prays prayers.

I am thankful for this church full of noise and laughing people who say *Happy Thanksgiving! Happy Thanksgiving!* and sing songs in Iñupiaq, which I like to hear even though I don't understand it.

When Thanksgiving is over, there are no more boxes full of frozen meat and *maktak* outside the church. The boxes that used to be outside are empty and the boxes people brought are full of food, all kinds of food, even fruit. Food for every family. Even the ones that don't got money to buy turkey.

Even the ones who don't got moms or dads.

December

Atikłuk

Aaka is sewing me something on the sewing machine. She calls it a snow shirt sometimes and an *atikłuk* other times. Snow shirt is Village English and *atikłuk* is Iñupiaq. It's the kind of clothes people wear for dancing; the kind like Sylvia's got, only mine's gonna be better. In school, girls wear *atikłuks* for the Christmas Program. Or fancy dresses, which I don't have. At the school Christmas Program kids sing Christmas songs and dance Eskimo dances and wear snow shirts and new shoes, too, if they have them.

My new snow shirt has a hood that fits just right and a big pocket and a ruffle with trim around the bottom and it's made out of red material with white reindeer on it. The *qupak* is green with one thin line of cobalt blue, same color as my bead. *Qupak* is what Aaka calls the trim. She guides the trim through the sewing machine with her fingers, bending her head down real close to see. And she makes it look just right, too, straight and smooth.

When Uncle sees my new Christmas *atiƚuk* with all its white reindeer, he goes, *Yum, yum. Reindeer soup,* and Isaac's eyes get big.

You can't eat Rudolph, Isaac announces. Uncle laughs.

Don't worry. Nobody gonna eat a reindeer with a red nose. Might make people sick, that kind.

But reindeer soup is yummy the way Aaka makes it. That's what I say.

THEY PUT ME right in front at the Christmas Program because I'm short and don't need to watch the others to know which dance steps to do when. The other girls are all watching *me*. I can feel their eyes on my back like warm hands. All of them except Sylvia. Sylvia's eyes do not feel warm. Sylvia's eyes feel like sharp hooks, poking me in the side.

Sylvia is not wearing an *atiƚuk*. Sylvia is wearing a pink dress like the kind Mom always say she's gonna buy me, but never does. A pink dress and Eskimo boots, that's what Sylvia's wearing, looking straight at me with a look that says she's better than everyone in the whole world, especially me.

But when we start dancing, I forget about Sylvia's pink dress and mean looks. When I dance, all I think about is the way the drums make us move together like we are all one big body. And I get proud when I see Aaka, smiling big in the front row where the elders sit, and I dance perfect, every step. No mistakes. Even though my braid is not perfect, my dancing is.

My braid is not like the way Mom makes it. It hangs down my back, swinging when I dance, moving back and forth to the beat of the drums, reminding me that Mom is not here.

Uncle is sitting next to Aaka in the front row, watching

me dance and saying things into Aaka's ears. Uncle is being Aaka's eyes, telling Aaka how good I dance, but I don't think Aaka needs eyes to tell about my dancing. I think Aaka feels the dancing without looking, just like me.

When we're done dancing, everybody claps and claps and I smile big at Aaka. I smile big at all the smiling faces, all the clapping hands. Rows and rows of people, smiling and clapping, their bodies moving in waves like the ocean.

Then, all of a sudden, all the sound seems to stop. Way far in the very back of the room, way past all the heads bobbing, right by the door where it's so dark you could hardly see anything, I think I see her—my mom.

I look at Aaka and Uncle and smile big. *Is it true?* I ask them with my eyes. Then I turn and look to the back of the room again, but she's not there.

Was I just imagining things in the dark again?

Now I'm standing up here feeling all alone, smiling so hard my throat hurts—the kind of hurt that comes just before you start to cry. Me, standing up in front of the whole clapping town, all alone, trying hard not to cry.

It feels like my mom is gone for good, stuck on the other side of a wall of ice, lost in a place where dancing is evil and no one ever smiles.

AFTER WE FINISH dancing and singing Christmas songs, Aaka's friends all crowd around me, patting my *atikłuk* and nodding at my new *kamaak* and saying *Aarigaa! Aarigaa!* But when they try talk to me in Iñupiaq, I don't understand. They are all smiling big at me and saying things in Iñupiaq, but all I could say back is *ii* and *quyanaq*. Nodding and smiling. And almost crying.

Ii. Quyanaq. Ii. Quyanaq.

Yes and thank you, yes and thank you.

I say it so much that it doesn't even feel like words anymore, just sounds. And the real words I want to say, the real Iñupiaq words, those are stuck way down deep inside my chest, so far down they don't make no sound at all.

A bunch of girls are standing around Sylvia, looking at her dress. The pink is very shiny and stiff and those girls all want to try touch it. Me too, but I don't say. I try not to even look, but I can't help it.

"From my dad," Sylvia tells the others. She says it so loud even Aaka turns to look.

Sylvia's dad is standing right next to her. You could tell he's her dad because he got her same mouth and is smiling big at everyone and holding hands with Sylvia and her brother.

Sylvia act like that shiny pink dress makes her queen of the world. And her dad acts the same way, puffing out his chest when he smiles, like he thinks he's boss of everyone.

Aaka and one of her friends are watching Sylvia's dad out of the corners of their eyes, frowning and muttering. They're talking about him in Iñupiaq, too, you could tell. And they are not saying good things, either. You could tell that, too.

Sylvia's dad has a scar on his cheek and does not look anything like the dad she drew for Thanksgiving, even if he is smiling. Sylvia's dad looks mean, just like Sylvia.

We walk home, across the village. The night is starry-bright and cold, and me and Isaac are glad Aaka can make warm parkas. We pull our ruffs up close to our faces and watch our breath puff out in little frozen clouds when we talk. Up in the sky the stars are breathing, too. You could see the star breath blowing across the sky in long smoky ribbons of color, appearing and disappearing. Like the sky is talking, too.

Northern lights, Aaka says, when Isaac asks.

I watch the way the northern lights flash on and off across the sky and I imagine them moving to the sound of a drum. Dancing back and forth across the sky. *Boom, boom, boom.* Watching them makes me wish I could dance with them, dance right out across the snow-covered tundra and under the twinkling sky, free as the wind.

Isaac watches the northern lights with his head cocked sideways like he's afraid they might try grab him. His eyes dart back and forth across the sky, nervous.

Mom said northern lights play ball with people's heads, he tells Aaka.

Aaka laughs. *Only kids who don't keep their hoods on*, she says.

Isaac pulls his hood up tighter.

I try to imagine the northern lights playing ball with peoples' heads. This makes me think about that scar on Sylvia's dad's cheek—I don't know why, it just does. What were Aaka and her friends saying about Sylvia's dad? That's what I want to know.

I can't understand, I tell Aaka. *I can't understand when they talk Iñupiaq.*

It's okay, Aaka says. *You will.*

January

Looking for My Mom

In school Miss Colato tells us to write about our holidays. She says to write like we're writing a letter to someone, telling them about it. I write a letter to my mom:

Dear Mom,

At the Christmas Program, I wore my new snow shirt that Aaka made. It has reindeer on it and it is red and green like Christmas. I stood right in the front row and I danced real good. Aaka said, "*Aarigaa!* You dancing like a real Iñupiaq." Real Iñupiaq dancing is different than the kind they do in Anchorage. Real Iñupiaq dancing is not bad like that kind.

Lots of people came to watch the Program. I even thought I saw you watching, but I was wrong. You weren't there.

At the Christmas Feast we have reindeer soup and *maktak* and I looked for you there, too, because I

know you like reindeer soup and *maktak* just like me.
I pretended you were sitting in the back row watching me use an *ulu*. I could use an *ulu* real good now.

When are you coming home?

Love,

Your Blessing

I had to use the Iñupiaq dictionary to spell the Iñupiaq words right. Miss Colato wrote *Bravo!* on my paper. *Bravo!* is how you say *Aarigaa!* in Spanish, which is the same as saying *Wow!* in English. When people do their best work, Miss Colato always writes *Bravo!* I like it when she does this, but if I ever get to be a teacher, I know what I will write—I will write *Aarigaa!* when kids do good.

Miss Colato says I am getting very good at translating from Village English into School English. She only changed a few things in my letter. She said *real* needs an *-ly* both times and *could* needs to be *can.* And she changed "we have reindeer soup" to "we had reindeer soup" because she said it already happened, so it's in the past. In School English you always have to separate things into past, present, and future—I don't know why. The way I see it, things don't always separate that easy.

Kirsten Johnson, whose mom is a teacher, says I have to change what Aaka said, too. She said Aaka is supposed to say: "You are dancing like a real Iñupiaq." But Miss Colato said I don't have to change the way my *aaka* talks.

She's right, too. The way my *aaka* talks is good the way it is, and nobody has to change it. That's what I think.

Kirsten Johnson said that's not what Miss Pickering said last year.

But we don't have Miss Pickering this year—that's what I tell Kirsten Johnson.

Bravo! No Miss Pickering.

That's what I say to myself.

Miss Colato says she will mail all our letters, and she made everyone read their letters out loud except for Sylvia. At first I thought that maybe Sylvia never wrote anything. But at the end of the day, right after the bell rang, Miss Colato put her arm around Sylvia and said, *Sylvia, I need you to stay for a few minutes, I'd like to talk to you about your letter, okay?*

Nobody else could hear this, nobody but me and Sylvia. All of the others are leaving, knocking into desks and each other in a mad rush to get out of the room. The hallway echoes with the sound of kids hollering and locker doors slamming. The look on Sylvia's face says I better get out quick, too.

None of your business, Sylvia's look says.

Miss Colato's look says the same thing, too, only nicer.

What is it, Blessing?

For a second, I don't know what to say. Then, without even thinking, I blurt it out: *How long does it take for a letter to get to Anchorage?*

Anchorage is quick, Miss Colato says. *Your letter will get there in just a few days.*

I stumble out of the room, embarrassed, running those words over and over in my mind: a few days, just a few days. Mom will read my letter in just a few days.

Going Back to Anchorage

My mom got my letter, all right. She calls to tell me. *Aarigaa*, she says. *You write real good, Blessing.* And I smile big because she is calling me Blessing, not *Sister* and not *Pakak. Blessing.*

Maybe I am.

My mom say I can go back home to Anchorage now. She win money at Bingo and she's gonna pay my ticket. She could pay Isaac's ticket next time, and Stephan is gone now, too. That's what my mom says.

I should be very, very happy, but all of a sudden I realize one hard thing: I don't want to go Anchorage, even if it means going back to Mom.

I don't *ever* want to go back to Anchorage, where everything turns bad, even dancing. I want to stay here with Aaka and have my mom come here, too. And that's exactly what I tell Mom, too.

For a long time there's no sound on the phone except silence. I don't say anything else and she doesn't say anything either. Both of us just sit there listening to the sound of each other saying nothing.

Bingo? I say, my voice hard and tight.

Blessing? Mom says finally, but I can't answer because I'm afraid I might cry.

Knock-knock, Mom says. Her voice sounds small and chirpy, like a toy bird, the kind you wind up.

I still don't say anything. The knock-knock door is closed tight and I don't want to open it. Not now. All I can think about is how I don't want my mom to go Bingo no more, because she always drink beer when she go Bingo. I don't say this because I don't have to. Mom knows.

I'm gonna quit, Nutaaq, she whispers.

I can't even remember the last time my mom called me by my Iñupiaq name.

I know, I say, without even thinking.

And I do, too—that's what I realize all of a sudden. Nutaaq knows that someday Mom's gonna quit drinking. Blessing isn't so sure, but Nutaaq knows.

Mom don't say anything else. The reason she don't talk is because she's crying, just like me. Mom don't make any sound when she cries, so how come I know? I can't say for sure, but I just do.

I hang up the phone feeling like I should do something, but there's nothing left to do. Nothing in the whole world. That's exactly how I feel. I go into the living room where Isaac is sprawled out on the floor playing with one small truck, running it backward and forward and making noises for it like a little kid. Which he isn't. Aaka's sitting on the couch, listening to the TV. At first I think she never even hear me come into the room.

Then she looks up and says, *So, how's your mom?* and something inside me snaps like a little red-hot firecracker of anger, sharp and clear. *You should know*, I want to say. *You're her mom.* But I don't say it.

How come you left her? That's what I do say. My voice feels sharp as ice.

Aaka looks up, confused, and for a second she looks totally blind, like she can't see a single thing.

Left who?

Mom! I say. *How come you left her with her aaka?*

I think I already know the answer. I know real well about why some moms can't take care of their kids; why some kids have to go live with their *aakas*. I just want to hear Aaka say it.

But what she says is not what I expect.

I was sick, Aaka says. *I got TB that time and they send me away.*

I'm so surprised by this, I don't know what to say. *Sick? They send people away for being sick?*

Aaka sighs. *I was gone a real long time. When they finally let me come home, your mama was all grown up and you were almost ready to be born. Your mama had quit calling me Mom by then. And when her aaka Nutaaq died, she just packed you up and left.*

Why? I ask.

Aaka looks at me with her sad, blind eyes and says, *Because.*

And Aaka says that word *because* the same way Mom

always says it, too. Like it's the beginning and the end of a sentence, both. *Because.*

Because there's things too hard to talk about, even for adults.

We never get along much after that, Aaka says. Her voice is so soft it's almost a whisper.

Ice Curtain

It is almost February and the sun is finally coming back. It's coming back today, while we're in school, and Miss Colato is happy. Miss Colato says she misses the sun more than anything. And pretty soon the ocean ice is going to open up and the whales will come back. That's what Uncle says.

I tell Miss Colato about the ice opening up and about the border in the ocean, too—the line no one could see. The one where people get shot. The one my great-great-aunt could never cross.

Miss Colato shows us a newspaper article about that same border. The newspaper calls it the Ice Curtain. I wonder why they call it that—is there really a curtain of ice out there? The newspaper says the Ice Curtain has melted. The Ice Curtain is gone, just like the Iron Curtain.

How could it melt when it's still winter and the ocean is still frozen? Kirsten asks. That's what I wonder, too. But I don't say it out loud because I am not rude like Kirsten. I know you're not supposed to argue with teachers.

It wasn't really there in the first place, Miss Colato says. *"Ice Curtain" is only a figure of speech.*

Figure of speech is the same as pretend. But people could still get shot if they crossed the Ice Curtain, even if it is only a figure of speech. Miss Colato says that used to be true, too, but not anymore. Now people can go right across it, no problem.

Outside the classroom window, at the edge of the sky, a line of bright pink and orange light is starting to grow. Ever since November the sun has been sleeping but now it's coming back. At first I could just barely see the top of its head, like a big ball of orange fire, but all afternoon I watch it get bigger and bigger and brighter and brighter, crossing up into the sky and covering everything with a pink and purple light. I get warm just watching it, even though I know it's still bitter cold outside, cold enough to make your ears turn white with frostbite just walking home. If you forget to wear your hood.

I don't forget mine. I'm out in the hallway after class, tying a scarf around my neck to hold my hood in place, when I hear somebody hollering. Someone big is hollering the F word. A lot.

Isaac hears it, too. He's standing against the wall like he got frozen there, afraid to even breathe. Isaac wants to hide, I could tell. I wanna hide, too—hide under a blanket like in my lemming story. Hide and holler out my name, my Iñupiaq name.

Come on, I say, grabbing Isaac's hand, pulling him away.

We are almost at the entrance to the school, ready to run

outside, when the door to the office flies open and a big man explodes out into the hallway, cussing like crazy. It's Sylvia's dad. He's dragging Sylvia by the arm.

NO WAY IN HELL! Sylvia's dad yells, yanking Sylvia's arm hard.

When he gets close we could smell the beer. Sylvia don't look at us at all. Sylvia don't look at anyone.

March

Good Things and Bad Things

I am trying to get things sorted out, good and bad. Some things sort out easy and some don't.

One good thing about my mom is she know how to braid hair all kind of ways and she likes knock-knock jokes and pizza. Aaka don't. The good thing about Aaka is she don't play Bingo and she don't drink beer. Mom does.

The good thing about Anchorage is they got big movies you can drive to in a car and trees that smell good. The bad thing is that people there are strangers and when they look at you they don't even see you, sometimes. Other times they look like they feel sorry for you. Or embarrassed. Or mad. They don't use their eyebrows like we do, to say yes. Their eyebrows always say no, frowning.

The best thing about the village is all the adults here say they your cousin or your auntie or your uncle or your *ataata* or your *aana* or your *amau*. Or your mom's classmate. And they always try hug you big, sometimes, too, and say how you look just like their favorite aunt.

The bad thing is there's no trees and no place to drive to in a car even if you have one, which we don't.

The bad thing about Isaac is he talks too much and always think he knows everything when he don't even know how to say thank you in Iñupiaq. The good thing is he stays close and holds my hand when strangers try look at us funny or uncles try hug too hard. Or a mean person hollers.

Uncle says we're Iñupiaq and Iñupiaq is best. Aaka says Eskimos don't brag. Uncle says they don't brag because they don't have to.

Quyanaq. That's how you say thank you in Iñupiaq.

I say thank you because Sylvia's dad is gone now—they take him away from the village and Sylvia's okay. Even if I don't say it out loud, I feel good about this, too.

Quyanaqpak.

April

Whale Understanding

T *hey giving out candy at Nusunginya's house!*
    That's what the CB radio says. It's a woman's voice, loud and full of static, making the CB in Aaka's kitchen buzz with excitement.

Come on over, kids! We got candy! Lots of candy!

They giving it out at Savik's and Akootchook's houses, too. Candy everywhere.

Whaling crews always give out candy before they go out whaling. They give candy to all the kids. Every time. That's what Aaka says. They give candy because they know the whale's gonna come to the crew that's good to people. Especially kids. That's what Uncle says.

A whaling captain can't be stingy, Aaka says. *A whaling captain has to take care of everyone.*

Especially old people and kids who don't have moms or dads. And moms who don't have no husbands.

Aaka knows all about whaling captains because that's

what her dad was, and my Ataata Joseph, Aaka's brother, too. Whaling captains.

The whales could hear real good, Uncle says. They hear everything we say, all the time, and they know right away if we say bad things.

They could hear people say *Good luck, good luck* to all the crews over and over on the CB. The sound of happy people makes the whales happy, too. Whales only come to places where people are happy. That's what Uncle says.

The crews have their sleds packed high with everything they need for whaling: white tents and stoves and caribou-skin mattresses to sleep on while they camp out on the white ice, waiting for whales.

The whalers all have new white parkas and new *kamaak*, too, and everything they have is clean, even the ice cellars, because that's the way the whales like it. Whales won't go to people who are dirty or lazy.

Nobody fights or says mean things. Especially not on the CB because they know the whales might hear.

I bet the whales don't go Anchorage, where my mom's at.

It's okay, Uncle says. *If we catch a whale we gonna share it with everyone all over the state. We gonna send some to your mom, too.*

MOM WENT BACK TO treatment. That's what Aaka says, when Isaac asks. Isaac cries because he thinks treatment is a place people go to when they're hurt. He's right, too. It is. But not the kind of hurt you could see right off, like a broken arm.

Uncle messes Isaac's hairs and says, *It's okay, guy, sometimes it takes a few times for treatment to work. Your mom gonna get fixed up good this time for sure.*

I'm thinking about Mom at treatment, watching out the window where big fat flakes of snow are falling down from the sky, slow as feathers. The whalers have been out a long time now, and I'm trying not to be jealous about the fact that Isaac got to go out to whale camp with Uncle but I had to stay home with Aaka. You are not supposed to be jealous during whaling season. Aaka doesn't say it, but I already know, watching the snow fall and listening to the CB. Which all of a sudden starts making lots of noise.

Heyheyheyhey! people holler on the CB.

Praise the Lord! an old lady's voice cries.

Ataata Joseph's crew caught a whale and now everybody, the ones in town and the ones out on the ice, are telling each other the news. That's what Aaka says. And now everyone is thanking the Lord and everybody else, saying congratulations about the whale. They are all talking in Iñupiaq, everybody talking together, talking so happy it sounds like the CB is laughing and singing all by itself.

Outside, people start to buzz back and forth on snow machines, pulling sleds out onto the ice to help the whalers. In the houses people are making doughnuts. Me and my *aaka* are making them, too. Frying so many Eskimo doughnuts in hot oil that the windows start to drip with steam and our stomachs get soft and full like bread dough.

Whales come to people who are generous. That's what Aaka says. Maybe the whale came to Ataata's crew because his crew gave out lots of candy to the kids. That's what I think.

They pulled the whale up onto the ice way offshore, and on the CB you could hear people sending messages back and forth from the ice to town, telling people what everybody's doing, ordering the things they need: more sleds and more people to help and more coffee to keep people awake. It takes a long time to prepare a whale. All night long people are working, never even sleeping. All night long the CB is chattering back and forth, happy happy happy. And at Aaka's house, even the walls are smiling. All the pictures of our whole big family, smiling. I never noticed before, how many of them are smiling. It makes me feel warm inside how they smile that way, like they all want to say *heyheyhey* about the whale, too.

I get to ride out to whale camp on my cousin's skidoo, ride right out onto the ice with its big blue-white chunks of icebergs. It's a long, bumpy ride. Two miles, Cousin says.

The whale camp is right on the edge of the water and over top of the water is the biggest sun I ever seen. A big orange sun, burning at the far edge of the ice like the ocean's made a bonfire.

Out at whale camp, Isaac is helping the men. He's dressed in the white parka Aaka made him and looking so grown up that for a second I almost don't recognize him. Everybody is busy working and calling to each other in Iñupiaq, and I can understand them—that's what I realize, all of a sudden: they are talking in Iñupiaq and I understand, just like Aaka said I would!

Maybe it's the whale that makes me understand.

June

Friendship Flight

School is over and summer is here and something very important is about to happen. The Ice Curtain is gone, and they gonna let Russian people fly to Alaska.

It's called a Friendship Flight and some of the people on it will be Eskimos, too, Siberian Eskimos. That's what the newspaper said. And some of them are coming to our village to visit us. They are coming for Nalukataq, the whaling festival, which is when we will celebrate my Ataata Joseph's whale.

We gonna welcome them at the airport. I got picked to be one of the welcomers because I'm in the dance group.

I'm wondering if my great-great-aunt Aaluk will be on the Friendship Flight. But Aaka says no, she won't, because she's too old. My great-great-aunt probably isn't alive anymore—that's what Aaka says.

But who knows? That's what I say.

JUST ABOUT the whole town is outside the airport watching the runway, waiting for that plane to land. Us welcomers get to wait right on the edge of the runway, right next to the people from Anchorage who are setting up cameras and microphones and getting ready to take pictures of the plane landing and of us in our *atikłuks* and *kamaaks*, and me holding my Eskimo yo-yo, waving.

The drummers are here, too, waiting to drum. They gonna drum and sing, to welcome the Russians, but we aren't gonna dance until later.

The sun is shining so hard we all squint our eyes, watching the sky, wanting to be the first to see the plane.

There it is! Isaac cries suddenly, and we all stare at the little black spot in the clouds, which is getting bigger and louder by the second.

The plane lands, kicking up dust in the sunshine, and the men start drumming as soon as they see the Russians walking down the steps. You could tell they are Russian because they look different—their clothes are different, too.

I am proud of the way our drums sound, welcoming the Russians to our village. And I'm proud, too, of the way the women's voices sound, strong as the wind, singing our songs.

There are twelve Russians, but only three of them look Eskimo: an old man, who is wearing a men's snow shirt, and another man who has his hand on the shoulder of a boy my age. All three of them have real smiles, the kind that make their eyes close. None of the others look Iñupiaq. The women have yellow hair, blue eyes, round faces, and skinny smiles. None of them look the way my great-great-aunt Aaluk would look. They shake hands and the old man bends down low and shakes my hand, too. He has a big necklace on underneath his snow shirt that makes a weird bump I try not to stare at.

The boy has discovered my yo-yo. He stands there, eyeing it. While the adults introduce themselves over and over, he keeps right on staring—looking at my yo-yo, then looking at me. And, finally, smiling.

You want to try? Yes? I say, raising my eyebrows, Eskimo-style.

He looks at me and smiles big. Even though he doesn't understand my words, he understands my eyebrows—I can see it in his face.

Then he raises his own eyebrows, too: *Yes.* He wants to try.

At first he only holds the yo-yo, running his fingers along the caribou-sinew string like he enjoys the feel of it. Then he swings it and swings it—just right, too. The polar bear fur balls fly round and round like little planets, sparkling in the summer sun, and the adults stop talking to watch. We are all standing there, by the sunny airport, listening to the *whir whir* of that yo-yo flying. Watching that Russian boy who knows how to use an Eskimo yo-yo, because he's Eskimo, too, just like me.

I think about all these Eskimos I never even knew existed, living on the other side of the ocean, just like Aaka said. Then I think about Eskimos living all around the top of the world, like it's another country, a country with its own borders, different from the ones they show on maps. Borders that have no Ice Curtains and no walls. This thought makes me feel good. Very good.

Eskimo Games

The Siberian Eskimo boy is named Petyr. He doesn't run fast, but he is good at the stick pull. That's what I find out when we start playing games. The Russian Eskimos are playing Eskimo games with us and they all know how, too, even the old man.

Eskimo games were made a long time ago by our elders to help keep people tough, because you have to be tough to live in the Arctic. That's what Uncle says. I think it's tougher to live in Anchorage, but I don't say this to Uncle.

We play in the field by the beach. The sun is high up in the sky and bright as a lemon. Even though it's already getting late, the sun stays up—the sun never sleeps anymore, just like us. All night long we play one-foot high kick, two-foot high kick, stick pull, and footraces. The only one I do is the footrace because I never learned all the others, and besides, I'm a good runner.

Petyr does the stick pull, which is a tug-of-war with a

stick using only your fingers. Petyr's hands are small but full of muscle, and his fingers don't let go of the stick, no matter how hard the other boy pulls. One by one all the others let go and drop out, but not Petyr. Petyr's skinny little arm is tough as a rope pulled tight. Right now he's in the last round of the stick pull, trying with everything he's got to beat the other kid, who's bigger than he is. The other kid is Sylvia's brother, who looks mean the same way Sylvia always looks mean. Sylvia's brother is very strong, too, and he's putting so much effort into trying to beat Petyr that his lips are pulled back and his teeth are clamped shut, like he's trying to bite something in half.

The stick pull could hurt a person's fingers bad, but those two boys refuse to let go. They sit on the ground across from each other, pulling so hard their fingers turn white. Neither one moves at all. They sit that way for a long, long time, looking like they just got turned into stone with their hands all twisted up together, both trying to outpull the other, neither one moving. Then, just like that, Sylvia's brother lets go and falls back. He rolls over and hits the ground hard with his fist.

Petyr reaches down, offers him his hand, and pulls him up. Then Petyr holds up the stick to show he's won and everybody claps and hollers.

When it's time for the footraces for girls, I go up and so does Sylvia.

Before I go to the start line, I take off my *atikłuk* so I could run faster. The blue bead is hanging around my neck, right there for everyone to see. Without even thinking, I reach up and hold on to it for just a second. I like the way it feels—

hard and warm, like it's alive. *Run fast. Faster than Sylvia. You can do it.* That's what the bead says.

We're standing on the field by the beach, waiting at the start line, all nine of us girls who are runners. There's a line laid out at the end of the field. We got to run to that line, then turn around and run back again. Sylvia is in the middle and I'm next to her. When I glance over at her, she glares at me. I glare right back.

The whistle blows and I take off, leaping into the race with one big jump. But Sylvia takes off even faster, shooting out ahead of me like a human bullet. For a second I want to sit right down and quit running because it feels like I already lost. Then I think about Sylvia and all her sister-cousins, snickering about my name, and suddenly it feels like my legs just got extra fuel. When we reach the turnaround, Sylvia and I are neck and neck, way ahead of all the others. Right when we turn, she glances over at me and glares at me like she thinks she could make me trip just by looking. Then she starts running harder. Me, too.

By the time we're halfway back to the finish line, I'm starting to get ahead of her. I can hear her breathing hard, just over my left shoulder. She's so close, I can *feel* her breathing. It feels panicky and even a little bit scared. I think she knows I got her beat.

I want to laugh at Sylvia just like how she always laughs at me, but when I look back at her, something weird happens: I see this look on her face that makes me feel, for just a second, like I'm looking at myself. It's a look that says she knows she's running all alone, running against a whole bunch of things she couldn't name, even if she wanted to.

Her mouth is clamped shut like she's shutting out every-thing in the whole world with just her jaw. A person can do that, too—I know.

This makes me think about Stephan. But when I think *Stephan*, a picture jumps into my mind: Sylvia's dad, drag-ging her out of the school by the arm, and Sylvia, her eyes rock-hard, refusing to look at anyone. And all of a sudden, I wish I had a sister, a tough, hard sister like Sylvia. For a frac-tion of a second, I'm even pretending that me and Sylvia *are* sisters, running together. Outrunning everyone else in the whole world. But in the time I'm thinking all this, Sylvia pulls ahead of me and leaps across the finish line.

We stand there together huffing and puffing, while the others cross the line one by one and I can't help myself—I look right at Sylvia and smile. Her eyes get real big for just a second and then she smiles, too, just a little. You can see she's trying not to, all right, but she smiles anyhow.

Maybe I let her win. Maybe not. Who cares?

Then I look over at Petyr to see what he thinks about the fact that I lost my race. But Petyr isn't looking at *me*. He and the old man are looking at my bead.

When I walk over to them, the old man taps my bead with one finger, like he's testing its power, and looks right into my eyes. Then he says something in Russian and smiles.

All of a sudden the Russian woman with yellow hair is talking at me.

He wants to know your name, she says. *He wants to know, are you the one named Nutaaq?*

I raise my eyebrows, surprised: *Yes*. Yes, I am. I'm the one named Nutaaq.

The old man nods slowly, speaking to the translator in Russian.

He wants to meet your parents, the translator says.

I frown. I haven't seen my mom in almost one whole year and I never even knew my dad. The word *parents* feels like a big bruise somewhere deep inside my chest. Without thinking, I take hold of my bead again.

Your family, the translator says slowly, like she thinks I don't understand. *He wants to meet your family.*

I look down, feelings packed up inside so hard I can hardly breathe. Then I look at Aaka and Isaac, sitting together at the edge of the field with Ataata Joseph. And I see my cousin Iñuuraq, too, and our aunties and uncles and cousins. And off in the back, the older ones—all our *ataatas* and *aanas.* And even Sylvia, standing there smiling at me for the first time ever, like she just learned how.

Then something warm as summer flows right through me and suddenly I'm smiling, too.

There's my family, I say, proud of them. I do have a family—a very big family. The old man is looking at my family, too, looking right at Aaka, and she's looking right back, like she could see everything I see, clear as day.

WE DANCE a welcoming dance for the Russians, and they watch close when we dance, following our every move, moving their bodies just a little, like they might know some of our songs.

When we dance the bird dance, the old man stands up and dances with us, because he does know it. He knows every motion and he moves just right, too. He makes himself look exactly like a bird when he dances, moving his head back and forth like how birds do when they're looking for food. Swooping down low with a fierce bird look that makes people want to duck and hide. And smile big.

I dance the last dance with the girls, but it feels different at first, like something is missing. I glance over at the others, to see what it is, but every one of them is dancing perfect, moving together like they're all part of the same body, even Sylvia.

When I look back at her, Sylvia isn't smiling, but she isn't glaring, either. She looks at me the same way she always look at her sister-cousins sometimes. And it's a friendly look, not a mean look.

That's when it hits me: I *am* one of the sister-cousins.

We're all dancing together under the soft blue summer sky: sisters, cousins, family. All.

Uyaġak

All the adults are sitting together at Aaka's house, trying to talk to each other even though they speak different languages. They're at Aaka's house because of me, because the old man made the translator introduce him to Aaka and Aaka said come eat with us. Now they're eating *maktak* with Aaka and the translator is sitting right there next to them, helping them understand each other. The old man can't speak English and he can't speak Iñupiaq, either.

How come he don't know Iñupiaq? Isaac whispers.

Isaac thinks Iñupiaq is the language of old people; that all the old people in the world speak Iñupiaq.

Nobody speaking this kind of Eskimo language anymore in Russia, the translator says. *They no longer living, the ones who are speaking it.*

I look at Aaka, at her frosty-window eyes and her small little mouth, speaking Iñupiaq words that sound like the wind. And suddenly I want to run over and put my arms around her to protect her. Protect her from what? I don't know, I just want to. But Aaka is smiling at the old man, offering him tea and Sailor Boy and jam. She doesn't look like she needs any kind of protection at all.

And when the old man tells Aaka his name, his Iñupiaq name, Aaka doesn't need anyone to translate. His name is Uyaġak.

That's an Alaskan name, Aaka says. *Means rock.*

The translator nods her head. *Yes. His mother is from Alaska,* she says. *This is why he travels with us.*

Aaka nods slowly, looking at Uyaġak for a very long time. Then she smiles and looks around like she could see everything as clear as day.

His mother is Aaluk, Aaka says.

And even though Uyaġak doesn't understand English, he nods his head quick because he hears his mother's name, Aaluk. He nods and nods at Aaka and says, *Aaluk,* over and over, smiling. Then he looks at me and says, *Nutaaq.* Aaka starts nodding her head and she's smiling, too. Soon, all of us are nodding and smiling, just like those little nodding toys. That's when I notice Uyaġak's necklace. It's been hidden under his shirt, but when he nods it makes his shirt move and I can see the color of it, all of a sudden: it's blue, dark blue.

Uyaġak looks at me and smiles. *Nutaaq,* he says. And he says it just right, too, like he's said my name a hundred times before.

Then, while I am still watching, waiting to see what else he's gonna say, he reaches into the neck of his snow shirt and pulls out his necklace—a whole string of blue beads, just like my one bead. Cobalt blue.

Aaluk's beads, Aaka says, looking right at me. Uyaġak is looking at me, too. And nodding.

The beads she promised her sister, Aaka says. *The beads she promised my mom, Nutaaq.*

Uyaġak holds the beads out, running his finger over them, one at a time, saying something in Russian. And even though I don't know the words, I understand what he's doing. He's naming the beads.

One bead for each person in our family, I say.

Uyaġak is saying the names now, too—I hear them. He says names in Russian and then he says the Alaskan names, too, saying them slower, like he's remembering something he learned a long time ago.

. . . Ubliuk, Nagazruk, Manu . . .

Manu. My mom's name. Her real Iñupiaq name. I take a deep breath.

Jukku, Amaġuq, Ayałhuq, Nuna, his old voice ticks.

Tupaaq, Aaluk . . . and Nutaaq.

When he says *Nutaaq*, he puts those beads right over top of my head and hangs them down around my neck. They feel warm and heavy against my chest, right next to my own bead.

I breathe out, slowly.

Happy, happy, happy.

That's the only word I can think of right now and it's not a big enough word, not even close. I think about how people might say *happy* in all the different languages in the world: Russian, English, Iñupiaq, Spanish . . . but I don't think those happy words, all stacked one on top of the other as high as the moon, could even begin to explain the way I feel.

We gonna have a real good Nalukataq this time, Aaka says,

her voice whispery, like she doesn't want to disturb all the good feelings. All the Russians look at her. I don't think they ever heard that word before.

Nalukataq is where they celebrate the whales, Isaac tells the Russians. Like he's been celebrating whales all his life. For real, neither one of us is exactly sure what Nalukataq is either until it happens.

Nalukataq

Nalukataq means *blanket toss.* The blanket is made out of sealskin—the same skins that used to be on the whaling boat. The people stand in a big circle, everybody holding on to the edges of the blanket, shaking it up and down together, to make the jumper go higher and higher. Sometimes, when the person jumping is real good, they even do somersaults. And throw candy.

The candy rains down over top of our heads and everyone, even the adults, dives into the sand to get a piece. Petyr and I stand together grinning, stuffing our mouths with Jolly Rancher candies.

Candik, Petyr says, proud of himself.

In the old days, Uncle says, they used the blanket toss to call the people back who got lost at sea. Today, it's brought lots of people back, I think. Today it's even brought our family back from Russia, sitting here on the beach with us, letting the whaling crews serve us special Nalukataq food, all day long.

When the afternoon plane comes, it swoops down low and dips a wing, waving at all of us—hundreds and hundreds of people, sitting together. And when the plane does that, a lot of the people jump up, waving right back. Me and Petyr wave, too.

It's time to serve the frozen *maktak* now, and even more people start coming, because everybody likes *maktak*. Petyr and me go sit with Aaka and Uyaġak. We sit down right when the whaling crews start getting together to stand in one big circle, holding hands and praying.

Where's Isaac? I ask Aaka.

Aaka frowns and nods at the circle. *Shhh*, she says. *They praying.*

There is a very old lady, one of Aaka's buddies, who is saying a prayer in Iñupiaq, thanking God for the whales. It takes a very long time to thank God for the whales but finally she finishes and everybody cheers loud. Cheering for *maktak*. Thankful.

People are still crowding in, looking for places to sit, when the servers start going out into the crowd with boxes full of *maktak*, frozen blocks, pink and white. Just before the servers get to us, Aaka leans down next to me and says, *Look over there by your uncle, Nukaaluga.*

I look where Aaka is looking, trying to see Uncle. More and more people are coming in, standing at the edges of the crowd, looking for their families.

All of a sudden, I see him. He's in the middle of the crowd, looking right at me. I have to look hard, because this time I am very sure that the person standing right next to him is Mom. But I'm afraid to believe my eyes because I know how they always play tricks on me sometimes.

But this time it isn't a trick. This time it really is my mom. She's standing there, at the edge of the crowd, smiling. Right next to Uncle, holding Isaac in her arms even though Isaac isn't a baby anymore and is way too big to hold like that. When she sees me she starts running, still lugging Isaac in her arms—half dragging him, and the two of them together look like a huge clumsy creature with arms and legs sticking out every which way. They look so funny I burst out laughing.

Petyr looks up and sees them and now he's laughing, too. *That's my mom,* I say.

It feels so good to say it that I want to say it over and over again: *That's my mom. That's my mom.*

Petyr smiles like he understands. *Yes*, he says.

And suddenly Mom is right there next to me grabbing me up and hugging me and reaching out and hugging everyone else, too. Trying to hug everyone all at once, our whole big family. Even Petyr.

Yes, I say. Or maybe I don't say it. Maybe it's just this big sigh of relief, like a breath I've been holding inside forever, that feels, when I finally let it out, like that single little word.

Yes.

Tavra

om fixes my hair in the kind of braid I like, the kind
that goes all the way round my head like a crown.

You looking pretty, Lady, Mom says.

I'm surprised to hear my mom call me Lady like that, but
when I look in the mirror I see what she means. I look older
now, not so much like a *Sister* or a *Pakak*. More like a *Lady*.
Which I almost am, anyhow. I'm thirteen, a teenager now.
Old enough for high school almost.

Mom looks older, too; you could see it in her eyes. Her
eyes look like she's not quite sure about things. Like maybe
she just woke up from a real bad nightmare and is still trying
to figure out what's real and what's not.

But there's one thing I have to know. *How come you never
use your name, Mom, your Iñupiaq name?*

Mom gets real quiet, like she's wondering about this, too.

Maybe it got lost somewhere, Mom says.

I look at her face in the mirror and see the new lines

around her eyes and the little wisps of gray in her hair and I think about how she smiled in that one picture from when I was a baby. Will she ever smile that way again? I wonder. It feels like there is a big wide ocean in between then and now. But we made it. We made it to the other side. That's what I think.

Mom fixes her own hair with the black wood hair clip Petyr's dad gave her, which is very shiny with bright-colored flowers painted on it. The dolls they gave us are made out of the same kind of shiny black wood. The dolls go from big and round to teeny tiny skinny, one inside the other, like how stories go, sometimes. Like how our stories and Russian stories fit together, one next to the other, like a puzzle, one big giant puzzle that makes a brand-new picture when it's done. A brand-new story. Or maybe it's an old, old story we never knew, me and Isaac.

It's the story of my great-grandma Nutaaq, and the story of me—Nutaaq. And it's the story of me, Blessing, too. It's the story of the beads that went back and forth from Russia to Alaska. And it's also Uyaġak's story, which started in Russia, and Aaka's, which started in Alaska. And mine and Petyr's, which just got started, right here in Alaska, started by one blue bead, dangling from a string around my neck.

Blessing's bead.

All of a sudden I know just what I got to do. My fingers find the string, the caribou-sinew string that holds my one bead. I take it off and stand there, for just a second, holding the bead in my hand. It feels alive and beating, somehow, like a tiny blue heart. Then I reach over and put the necklace around Mom's neck, real careful. Mom looks down and wraps her fingers around the bead, like she's surprised to find it there. Like maybe it been there all along and she just now discovered it.

Nutaaq's bead, she whispers, standing there in front of the mirror, holding it. But her eyes are not looking into the mirror. Her eyes are looking somewhere else, somewhere far away. Like holding the bead is making her remember things. Good things.

Aaka says people don't think those beads got power anymore, but people are wrong. This one bead has lots of power. Enough to bring our Russian family and our Alaskan family back together again. Enough to bring my mom back home again. And me, too.

I'M REMEMBERING that story, now, the one about the lemming hiding under a sealskin and thinking how big he is. Thinking that the edge of the sealskin is the edge of the sky. How would he feel if somebody pulled up the sealskin to show him just how big the world *really* is? He'd be scared, probably, but only for a second. Then he'd race off down the beach, totally free, running right off into a brand-new story.

Maybe that's how it is. Maybe every time you lift the edge of the sealskin, you see another story.

This one is my story, mine to tell any way I want, because I am Nutaaq, the one who tells stories. And that's how stories are, sometimes sharp as ice and sometimes as round as a single bead.

And sometimes, both.

Tavra.

Author's Note

Although *Blessing's Bead* is fictional, much of what I've written about is based on real events. In 1986 I was a public radio reporter covering a meeting of an international organization representing the Inuit people of Alaska, Canada, Greenland, and Russia. It was the tail end of the Cold War and the Russian Inuit were attending for the first time. I interviewed an older Yupik Eskimo woman from Alaska's St. Lawrence Island who remembered how the Siberian Inuit used to visit her village every summer when she was a young child. She told me that many of the people of the region had intermarried and gone to live in Russia, but due to the "Ice Curtain"—the closed border separating Alaska from Russia—these people had remained separated from their families for over forty years. She left me with a haunting image I've never forgotten: old women, standing on the western shore of the island, gazing toward Russia with tears in their eyes, missing their Siberian relatives. This image gave birth to *Blessing's Bead*.

Nearly twenty years later, when I finally began to write this story, I placed it on an Iñupiaq Eskimo island farther north than St. Lawrence Island, which is Yupik Eskimo. I set the story within the Iñupiaq region for largely personal reasons: I married into the Iñupiaq culture and know it well. But my choice of setting is also historically accurate. Although St. Lawrence Island is Yupik, several smaller islands to the north, including King Island and Little Diomede Island, are Iñupiaq. Alaska's Little Diomede Island, in fact, is only a few miles distant from Russia's Big Diomede Island. During the Cold War, the Iñupiaq living on Big Diomede were relocated to Russian communities on the mainland. Historians report that the last Russian Iñupiaq still able to speak the Iñupiaq language was a woman who died in the late 1970s. Perhaps this woman originally came from Alaska, like Aaluk in my story.

The great trade fairs, like the one at Sheshalik, near Kotzebue, in the opening of the book, were traditionally held in several regions of Alaska. The Sheshalik fair is reported to have attracted over two thousand people annually, including boatloads of Siberians who traded brass pots, tea, tobacco, reindeer skins, and beads, similar to Aaluk's blue beads. An elder who participated in a trade fair as a child remembered the joyful sound of the drums, heard from a distance, just as Nutaaq heard them.

Maniilaq, the Iñupiaq prophet, was a real historical figure, as was Uyaġak, the preacher. Maniilaq did in fact predict the coming of the white people and Christianity and he also made a number of other striking predictions, including one about "boats powered by fire" that would one day fly the skies.

Reindeer herding was an industry introduced into Alaska in the late 1800s, when the United States government brought Siberian reindeer and reindeer herders into the Iñupiaq community of Kinegan, or Wales, Alaska. The project was spearheaded by a Presbyterian missionary, Sheldon Jackson, to provide Alaska's Native peoples with a livelihood, supplying food for the growing numbers of commercial whalers who were coming into the region and who were sometimes stranded there during the winter, straining the food supplies of their Iñupiaq hosts.

The worldwide Spanish influenza epidemic of 1918 devastated Alaska and did, in fact, leave many Native villages empty, killing thousands. It is referred to by the Iñupiaq of Kawarek (Nome) as the Fourth Disaster. The forced marriage of survivors is based on an incident recorded by the Presbyterian missionary Henry Greist.

"The-place-where-they-hunt-snowy-owls," which Tupaaq and Nutaaq are preparing to return to at the end of Book I, is a translation of Ukpiaġvik, the traditional name of Barrow, Alaska, the northernmost community in Alaska.

The reader is asked to understand that in Book I, Nutaaq and her family speak Iñupiaq, whereas the characters in Book II speak a dialect known as Village English.

The Friendship Flights between Russia and Alaska did in fact happen in the 1980s, although none came as far north as Barrow—my hometown. In the years after 1986, however, the Siberian Inuit have visited Barrow many times, and we always enjoy watching them dance.

The names used in this story are, for the most part, actual names. Every Iñupiaq name comes with its own family and regional ties and its own history. Nutaaq, Aaluk, and Tupaaq are names used in Barrow and not likely to be found as far south as the island where the story begins. I used them because Nutaaq and Aaluk's father's family, like Tupaaq's, was originally from Barrow. It was common, in the old days, for Iñupiaq hunters and their families to travel widely throughout western Alaska, so there are many cross-regional ties, even today.

But I use these names for another reason as well. Nutaaq and Aaluk are my daughters' names and thus I feel I have permission to use them. Permission is needed because the beliefs about naming are culturally significant. Family history is remembered through names and it is believed that when a child is given a name, part of the spirit of the relative who last held that name remains tied to it. This belief lies at the core of my story: Aaluk and Nutaaq, the two sisters separated by marriage, the great epidemic, the Cold War, and, ultimately, death, are not separated forever. Since their names remain linked in memory, their story will continue to echo from one generation to the next in remarkable ways if one listens closely.

While I was working on this book, my mother died. And although I dearly wish she could have lived to see the finished book, I know that like the story of Aaluk and Nutaaq, my mother's legacy lives on. It lives through me and also through my own daughters, one of whom, Aaluk, is also named Susan, after my mother.

Iñupiaq Glossary

Pronunciation guide: Iñupiaq sounds are difficult for the English language speaker. I have tried, for the sake of the reader, to give what I hope is an easy-to-understand guide. Please keep the following in mind:

$\dot{g}$ is guttural and has a slightly rolled sound, sometimes sounding like "aga."

ŋ sounds like "ing."

ñ is like the same character in Spanish: mañana.

ł is an *l* made with the sides of the tongue rather than the tip of the tongue.

ḷ is like the double-*l* in "million."

Names
Aaluk (*ah*-luke)
Manu (*mah*-new)

Nutaaq (new-*tahk*)
Tupaaq (too-*pahk*)
Uyaġak (*oo*-ya-gwahk)

Words
aahaaliq (ah-*haa*-lick): duck.
aaka (*aah*-kah): grandmother.
aana (*aah*-nah): great-aunt (currently); grandmother (traditionally).
aarigaa (aah-thėe-*gaah*): an exclamation expressing delight, meaning "Wow! Nice!"
aġviq (*ahga*-vick): bowhead whale.
amau (ah-*mau*): great-grandparent; great-grandchild.
Amiġaiqsivik (ah-me-*guyk*-see-vik): the-time-when-the-caribou-antlers-shed-their-velvet (August).
araa (ah-*thah*): an exclamation showing dismay, meaning "Too much!"
ataata (ah-*taah*-ta): great-uncle.
atikłuk (ah-*tick*-luke): a decorative shirt made in the style of a parka cover, also called a snow shirt.
cigaaq (see-*gahk*): slang for cigarette. Also spelled *sigaaq*.
iglu (*ig*-loo): house.
Iġñivik (ignyee-vick): the-time-of-birth (June).
ii (ee): yes.
iiqinii (ick-qi-*knee*): exclamation expressing fear.
Iñupiaq (*inyou*-peeahq): of the real people (North Alaskan Eskimo); the language spoken by the North Alaskan Eskimos.
kamaak (*cah*-mahk): a pair of boots.
Kawarek (cah-*war*-eck): traditional Iñupiaq name for the region of Nome, Alaska.

kik (keek): an exclamation meaning "Come on! Try hard!"

Kingigin (*keng*-ee-gen): traditional Iñupiaq name for Wales, Alaska.

kitta (*kee*-tah): an exclamation meaning "Let's get going!"

kiuġuya (*keyu*-goo-yah): the northern lights, or aurora borealis, said to be spirits that play ball with people's heads.

maktak (*muck*-tuck): whale skin with blubber.

Mauraġaraġaq (*mau-ra*-gara-gaq): a game played on the ocean, jumping from one piece of floating ice to another.

mikigaq (*micky*-gahk): a mixture of fermented whale meat and *maktak*.

Nalukataq (nah-*lu*ka-tuck): blanket toss (the whaling festival usually held in June, after spring whaling season ends).

naumi (*now*-me): no.

niġliq (*ni*ga-lick): goose.

Nippivik (*nip*py-vick): the-time-when-the-sun-sets (November).

nukaaluga (new-*kaah*-lew-gah): my little sister.

pakak (*puh*-kuck): someone who gets into mischief rummaging through things.

paniqtaq (puh-*nick*-tuck): dried meat or fish.

qavsiraq (*qahv*-see-ruck): whale blubber, eaten frozen.

quaq (quo*ahk*): frozen raw meat or fish.

qupak (*coo*-puck): decorative fancy parka trim.

quyanaq (*qwee*-yah-nuck): thank you.

quyanaqpak (*qwee*-yah-nuck-puck): thank you very much.

Sheshalik (she-*shaw*-lick): traditional name for an inlet near Kotzebue.

Siqiñġiḷaq (see-kiny-*gee*-lyaq): the-time-when-there-is-no-sun (December).

Siqiññaatchiaq (si-kin-*nyaht*-cheeahk): the-time-of-the-bright-new-sun (January).

tavra (*tahv*-ruh): that's it; the end.

Tiŋŋivik (*tingy*-vick): the-time-when-the-birds-fly (September).

tuttu (*toot*-too): caribou.

uii (oo-*ee*): an exclamation expressing joy, used by men while dancing.

Ukpiaġvik (ook-pee-*aga*-vick): the-place-where-they-hunt-snowy-owls; traditional Iñupiaq name for Barrow, Alaska.

uksi (*ook*-see): to sample, try, or taste.

ulu (*oo*-loo): traditional Iñupiaq woman's knife.

unipkaat (oo-*nip*-cot): legends, old stories, fables, myths.

uqaluktuat (oo-qah-*luk*-tooaht): true stories, accounts of events that happened during the past two or three generations.

uumaa (oo-*mah*): an exclamation meaning "Hey, you! Don't!"

Acknowledgments

I would like to thank the Society of Children's Book Writers and Illustrators for supporting my work on this book through a Work-in-Progress grant, and my family for their love and support, especially my husband, George Saggana Edwardson, oral historian extraordinaire. I also extend my gratitude to my colleagues at Vermont College of Fine Arts for their invaluable input: Louis Hawes, who saw the novel hidden within a picture-book manuscript; Ellen Levine, who always believed in me; Tim Wynne-Jones, who gave me wings when I most needed them; and Marion Dane Bauer, who taught me how to fly. Thanks, too, to my patient and perceptive writing partner, Jane Buchanan, who along with Tod Olson, Adrienne Ross, and Karmen Kooyers helped me breathe life into this story, and to Rene Colato Lainez, for letting Miss Colato use his name. I would also like to thank Dr. Edna Ahgeak MacLean for her help with the Iñupiaq glossary. And a final thanks to my editor, Melanie Kroupa, for her gentle hand and clear vision.